A Beth-Hill Novel:
Karen Montgomery Series:
Capture

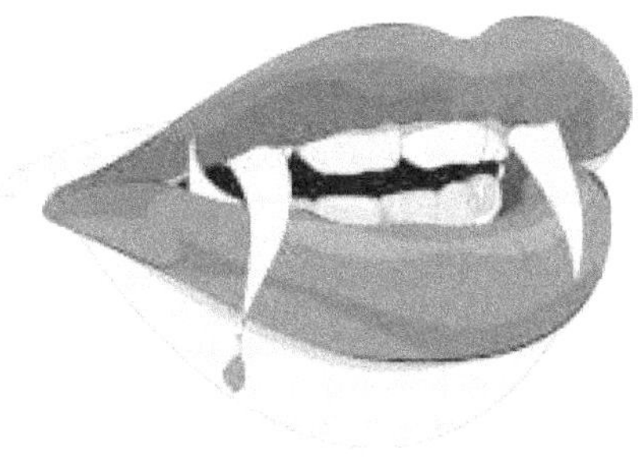

By Jennifer St. Clair

Writers Exchange E-Publishing
http://www.writers-exchange.com

Beth-Hill Novella: Karen Montgomery Companion Story: Russ' Story: Capture

Dedication

To Ethan

PART 1

Chapter 1

Vampire hunters have only two rules. The first one is to always get your quarry; the second never to mix business with your personal life. In fact, it was recommended not to even have a personal life, because if the vampires got wind of your mundane persona, your family members would be next on the list to die.

Russ knew this. He'd known this ever since he joined up with the Hunters at the tender age of eighteen. He'd known this when he first met Naomi. He'd known this when they dated, and eventually married, and through the birth of their daughter, Rosemarie.

But now, stuck in Southern Kentucky with no backup nearby and a nest of vampires somewhere in the vicinity, with Naomi refusing to speak to him--she'd fled to her parents' house with the baby--Russ fingered the photograph he'd taped to the dashboard of his van and sighed. Sometimes he hated the second rule.

He'd been chosen for this assignment because he was very, very good at his job. And he knew this with no sort of overblown sense of his own importance; he knew he was good at his job. That went without saying. And he also knew that he was the best person for this particular job, too.

If only...Russ closed his eyes and drummed his hands against the steering wheel. He had to concentrate. He could not think of Naomi and the baby now.

The steady beeping of one of the lights on the dashboard caught his gaze, and he realized that while he had been distracted, his quarry was on the move. Eyes glued to the computer display on the passenger side seat, he watched as a red dot emerged from the house he couldn't see and started walking up the driveway.

His palms were damp with sweat. He realized, suddenly, that he was far too nervous about this, even though unearthing such a large nest of vampires might mean he'd end up in the record books. Especially if he could pull this off.

His quarry kept moving, strolling almost, and Russ watched until the red dot was only forty feet away. The driveway was just past the stand of trees he'd hidden his van behind; only a quick dash through light underbrush and nothing more. Russ glanced at the dashboard; the same light beeped, indicating the presence of only one vampire, no more, no less.

A piece of cake, really. The accumulation of weeks of work, yes, but almost disappointing in its simplicity.

He grabbed his bag. Opened the driver's side door, leaving everything else behind. The van was sheathed in wards; no vampire would be able to detect it.

He didn't count on the fact that there might be humans with the vampires, or that his particular talent with technology might not be as rare as the Hunters claimed.

Russ took two steps away from the van and something...something exploded around him; a trap, he realized, but not a trap he could escape. A sticky mess of magic and energy from the electric lines spread in a deadly web of humming magic around him, effectively scrambling any sort of defense he might be able to muster. He tried, he had to try, but the resulting backlash brought him to his knees.

He dropped his bag, and knelt there on all fours, desperately trying to focus on something he could use. There was dirt under his fingers, but dirt wouldn't help him; there were leaves; he didn't realize that the net had drawn close around him until it latched onto his arm. He screamed as it wrapped around him like a particularly nasty choking weed; it had him helpless in the breath of an instant and he could do nothing to save himself.

The thought that he'd never see Naomi or Rosemarie crossed his mind and vanished under an onslaught of pain.

"Niles, stop."

He recognized that voice. His quarry. Watched as the vampire picked up his bag, its contents scattered on the ground when he dumped it out. Along with stakes and bottled garlic and holy water, his quarry tossed a small black button on the ground in front of Russ; back in the van, the red dot would be right in front of his nose now.

He tried to breathe, but the spell held him fast, choking off everything, including breath. Black dots danced in front of his eyes.

"Niles!" The vampire snapped the word, or the name, Russ supposed, and the relentless pressure eased up a bit. Not enough to speak, and he still couldn't move, but he could breathe now, barely, in faint, shallow gasps.

And a boy, also familiar, his hair a bit longer than fashion currently allowed, dressed in a t-shirt and torn jeans, stepped out of the trees and glared down at Russ.

At least he could understand being double-crossed. But how had the boy hidden his talent?

"Bring him," the vampire said, and turned away with the empty bag in his hand. He let it fall; crumpled onto the ground, and then someone grabbed Russ' arms--two someones, both vampires. And they lifted him up, effortlessly, and one said to the boy, "Do you think you could let him walk, at least?"

"He's not likely to know how to do magic with his toes," the other added, and Russ felt something release around his legs; he kicked out, or tried to--an automatic response--and the strangling pressure returned tenfold.

"Niles," his quarry said sharply. And then, to Russ, he said, "If you swear you will not attempt to escape, I'll allow you to walk. You have my word you will not be harmed."

But it was too late, even to laugh at the thought of trusting a vampire's word. Russ felt blackness rise up to claim him, heard the vampire growl at Niles again, and felt absolutely nothing, for a blessed space of time.

Russ woke, much later, to find he lay in a bed, not in a dungeon, or in a coffin, or on a floor, or anywhere uncomfortable at all. A perfectly normal, mundane bed, with white sheets and a comforter that had probably been purchased at a department store. His head lay on a feather pillow. The last time the sheets and pillowcase had been laundered, someone had used lemongrass scented detergent.

He turned his head. There was a vampire sitting in an upholstered chair, green upholstery, his mind supplied. An elegant paisley pattern that almost matched the comforter...less than five feet away. Russ' mind tried to convince him that he'd be able to launch himself at the vampire before it could move, but he had no weapons, and even he couldn't kill a vampire with his bare hands.

And he wasn't quite sure he could move.

The vampire was reading a book. Russ couldn't see the title because the vampire's hand was blocking it, but it was something by Nelson DeMille. And the vampire seemed to be wholly absorbed in the story.

"I know you're awake," the vampire said before Russ could speak, or try to move, or do anything but stare. He placed a bookmark, an actual bookmark, to save his place (vampires didn't dog-ear books?) and closed it. Folded his hands, and laced them across one bent knee.

The vampire wore human clothes, of course; they usually did. And he seemed to be about twenty; brown hair, slightly wavy. Green eyes. Pale skin, of course. Russ had never been so close to one without a weapon at hand, however. It wasn't a pleasant feeling.

"My name is Ethan," the vampire said calmly, as if discussing the weather with an acquaintance. "Your name is Russell Moore."

That they knew his name wasn't shocking; that Russ recognized the *vampire's* name left him stunned. He licked his lips. "Ethan Walker?"

"Welcome to my home," Ethan said, and picked up something from the table beside his chair. "Here. I think this is yours."

The vampire held out what Russ assumed was a piece of paper, at first. But then he realized it was the photograph of Naomi and Rosemarie, slightly singed on one corner, but otherwise intact.

He hadn't remembered taking it with him. Or had they found it in his van? Had they...

Ethan smiled, almost pitying. "You've been unconscious for less than three hours," he said. "We're not *that* good." There was no threat in his voice; no sign at all that he was lying. "And I can read your emotions quite easily, Mr. Moore. You can't access your talents here; Niles made sure of that."

"You...you killed..." Quite a large piece of Russ' mind kept shouting at him to shut up, but he couldn't stop himself from speaking.

"No. Not me," Ethan said. "No one here, actually, although we *do* know the identity of the one you seek."

Russ *was* after all, on a murder investigation. And the murderer was definitely a vampire. And all signs had pointed directly to Ethan Walker, who was--although Russ now doubted his sources--the leader of this particular nest of vampires.

Desperately, Russ tried to wrest his mind back to coherence. He saw that the vampire still held the photo out to him; he reached out to take it and realized that his hand was shaking.

Ethan didn't comment on it, although he couldn't have missed it. "Are you hungry? Thirsty?"

Russ stared at him. He wasn't used to this; not at all. Vampires were the enemy. If you were captured by the enemy, you died. There were no prisoners; no second chances. None at all. If they didn't kill you right away, then they made you into a vampire.

How would he know if they had?

"You're still human," Ethan said, as if Russ had spoken that question out loud. "You're still Russell Moore, Vampire Hunter. That hasn't changed."

"What has?" Russ asked before he could stop himself.

"The fact that you're here, with us," Ethan said calmly. "And that you haven't--in truth--been harmed."

"That spell...you count that as *unharmed?*" Russ asked. He wrestled with the sheets and the comforter for a moment, trying to sort out his arms and legs, then gave up, glaring at Ethan. "*Unharmed?*"

"Nothing a little rest won't cure," Ethan declared. "I'll have someone bring you something to eat." He stood; Russ had to steel himself not to flinch back. Vampire hunters did not flinch.

Ethan smiled briefly. "You'll feel better in the morning," he said. "I swear it."

"What will happen in the morning?" Russ asked, and felt something curious twist through his chest. After a moment, he realized it was fear.

"We'll talk," Ethan said. "Now get some rest."

Russ never knew if the vampire put him to sleep with some sort of suggestion or if he truly was tired enough to close his eyes and fall asleep in the middle of a nest of vampires by himself. But he felt his eyes slip shut; felt weariness tug at consciousness, and he was drifting again, in an endless sea of darkness. And for a little while, he was at peace.

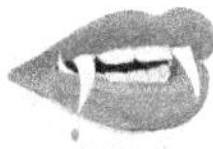

"Someone" was a child, around seven years old, thin and poised, her hair combed neatly and pulled back into two braids on either side of her head. There were no adults with her; no sign that anyone watched her from the door.

Russ could have overpowered her in an instant; could have taken her prisoner and demanded to be set free. He *could* have done all of that, but without his talent, he was at a disadvantage. Attempting to escape, now, without any understanding of Niles' spell or how to break it would be suicide.

And this girl, this child, was not a vampire.

So he sat up, vaguely surprised that he could, and pushed back the covers and swung his legs over the side of the bed while she watched. He still wore his own clothes. He still couldn't feel Niles' spell. Did it *exist?* Or had the vampire--had Ethan--been bluffing?

"Mama made you breakfast," the girl said softly, nervously. "And Uncle Ethan asked me to bring it to you."

Uncle Ethan?

"Thank you," Russ said, because he had no reason not to be polite.

The girl scurried out, leaving him alone with a tray of food and a host of unanswered questions.

In stocking feet, Russ stood and shuffled over to the tray. There was orange juice to drink, in a glass pitcher. Silverware wrapped in a napkin. A fork, a spoon...a *knife?*

Numbly, Russ waved his hand over the food, buttered toast, scrambled eggs, bacon, pancakes, and with what smelled like real maple syrup, too. And he murmured the familiar spell to detect poison, or drugs, and nothing happened.

The *spell* worked; that wasn't the issue. The spell worked. Which meant...

Without turning around, he said, "What do you want from me?"

"That would be the question, wouldn't it?" Ethan asked from the doorway. "How do you feel?"

Russ glanced back at him. "Dizzy," he said, and picked up the knife. "What did you do to me?" He knew Ethan hadn't missed his movements; deliberately, he picked up a piece of toast and spread jelly across the melted butter.

Even before he'd taken a bite, he realized he was ravenous.

"It was Niles' spell," Ethan said, almost apologetically. "He didn't realize it would affect you the way it did..."

"How did it affect me?" Russ asked, and sat down, because the chair looked more inviting than the floor. "Why am I so dizzy?"

"You've been unconscious for two days," Ethan said simply. "You stopped breathing twice before we realized what had happened. At first, we thought you'd taken something. Please accept my apologies."

Russ sat and chewed on the toast for a moment in silence, considering this. He selected another piece, ate it, too, and then, because he had nothing better to do, poured himself a cup of orange juice.

He felt off-balance and strange. Dizzy, yes, but also oddly accepting, as if some part of his body realized that he'd been unconscious for two days and had already accepted that fact.

"You thought I'd taken something, like what?" Russ asked.

"The Hunters are known for their prowess with poisons," Ethan replied. "It would make sense that you might be inclined to kill yourself instead of listening to what I have to say."

"You're not that boring of a speaker," Russ said absently, and then, hopefully, "Do you have any coffee?"

"Coffee?" Ethan asked.

"Caffeine?" Russ countered. "*Not* tea? I mean, I'll drink tea, but I *need* coffee."

"I'll...ah...see what we can do," Ethan replied, and vanished from the doorway.

Leaving it open. Interesting. Russ ate the rest of the food, except for the bacon, drank another glass of orange juice, and watched the door. After a few minutes, he stood up and wandered into the bathroom that adjoined the bedroom; when he emerged, there was a thermos of hot water on the table with a mug and a stack of those coffee teabags, which were only a step up from actual tea in Russ' opinion.

Russ made a cup without checking if it was poisoned; if Ethan wanted him dead, he would have been dead already. And he sat back down in the chair and closed his eyes and drank; felt the fuzziness finally lift from his mind.

"You do realize Niles had to break the spell?" he asked without opening his eyes.

"You do realize you're surrounded by vampires, and you'd have a very hard time escaping if you tried?" Ethan asked, again from the doorway.

"'Very hard' doesn't mean impossible," Russ said, and wondered why he wasn't afraid. "Why am I here?"

"A few of the others thought I should let you die," Ethan said. "You are well within your rights to retaliate. I am asking that you do not."

Russ opened his eyes. Stared at Ethan for a moment, then motioned to the other chair. "Please, sit down. Don't hover." And then, when Ethan didn't move, he asked, "You would accept the word of a vampire hunter?"

"If you would accept the word of a vampire," Ethan said. "No one here will harm you. We only wish to be left in peace."

Peace was such a funny word. So far-reaching; so impossible. "The Hunters and the vampires will never know peace," he said.

"But what about Ethan Walker and Russell Moore?" Ethan asked.

"You are asking me to betray--"

"No." Ethan stepped inside the room and closed the door. "I'm not asking you to betray anyone or anything. Your ideals remain intact. You are under no compulsion to kill each and every last one of us here; the only reason why you're here is to find a murderer. Am I right?"

Russ thought about it for a moment. "Technically, yes. Except for the fact that all of my evidence points towards *you* as the killer."

"All of your evidence is circumstantial," Ethan said. "And we've already found the real murderer."

Russ sat up straight. "You have? Where is he?"

"All in due time," Ethan said, and folded his arms. "I would have your word, if you will give it to me."

"That I stay silent about you?" Russ asked. "I can't do that. You might as well kill me and be done with it; I cannot--and *will* not--betray the Hunters."

"I'm not asking you to," Ethan said patiently. "I'm only asking that you not retaliate against us. This house. Here. Me. My family. And in exchange you will leave here alive with your murderer in hand. Your task will be complete. And you can see *your* family again. As I wish to see mine."

"They will still see that as a betrayal," Russ said, and knew that to be truth, deep down in his heart. He carefully set down the mug. Was the knife sharp enough? He would soon find out. "You see, the Hunters exist for one goal and one goal alone; to eliminate vampires from this world. If I were to ignore what I know; if I dared pretend I didn't know you are here, then who would I betray next? My family? No." He picked up the knife; carefully wiped it free of jelly. "I can no more ignore your presence than I can pretend my wife was wrong when she said there was no room in my life for her or our daughter."

There were tears in his eyes now, blurring Ethan's face. He stood up and faced the vampire. "You don't understand. Just by speaking to you I'm already compromised. I'm already lost."

He sliced the knife across his wrist, or tried to, but the vampire was there in an instant, tearing the knife away; blocking the spells Russ threw at him until finally, his temper snapped and he snarled in frustration and lifted Russ up with one hand.

"I offered you your *life*!"

Russ closed his eyes. "My life does not matter."

"Not even to your daughter, who will grow up never knowing her father?" Ethan asked, and let him fall back down.

"Perhaps it's better that way," Russ whispered, and opened his eyes when Ethan didn't reply.

The little girl stood in the doorway, eyes wide, one hand on the doorknob. Ethan had turned to face her. Russ could have picked up the knife; could have stabbed Ethan Walker in the back; could have then taken the girl hostage; he could have done these things. He had done them before. Well, not to a human child. But he could have.

"Emily?" Ethan asked.

"Aden said if you're not going to bring him soon, he's going to go back home," the girl reported. "Because he thinks you are stalling."

She sounded as if she was quoting the last part.

"I imagine he does," Ethan said dryly. "Tell him he can wait a few minutes more."

"Who is Aden?" Russ asked. "And I thought *this* was your home." And then, before Ethan could reply, he said, slowly, "This *isn't* your home."

"No, of course not," Ethan said. "Do you think I'd be stupid enough to keep a live Hunter in my own house?"

Emily giggled at his tone of voice.

Russ didn't feel much like giggling. "Then what do you want from me?" he asked, almost plaintively.

"Peace between us," Ethan said immediately. Seriously. As if that was the simplest thing in the world to request.

"You're crazy," Russ said before he could stop himself.

"Perhaps." Ethan didn't seem to be disturbed by the prospect. "But if no one ever tries, then how will something so impossible ever be achieved?"

There were no words to refute that kind of logic. Russ stared at him, then at Emily, and wondered if the vampires had scary stories about the Hunters as the Hunters had scary stories about the vampires. Every assignment he'd ever been on had been justified; at least on paper. He'd never come across a nest--a *house*--a family, like this one before.

He licked his lips. "*Uncle* Ethan?"

"Emily is my sister's daughter, yes," Ethan said mildly.

"And you let her come here? You left her alone with *me*?"

"I had hopes that you wouldn't murder a human child, even if she lives in a vampire's household," Ethan said.

"But I could have," Russ whispered, appalled that he had even entertained the thought.

"But you didn't," Emily pointed out. "You didn't even try."

"But I thought about it," Russ told her, and hunched over with his head in his hands. "I considered it."

"And yet you didn't act," Ethan said. "Why not?"

"I don't know." Russ whispered the words and found them wanting. It wasn't that he didn't *know;* he couldn't bear to examine his reasons for hesitating. For not doing exactly what they had to expect him to do. He raised his head. "Emily is your *sister's* daughter? But I thought you were born a vampire."

"I was," Ethan said, amused. "You Hunters don't know everything about vampires."

"That's quite obvious," Russ said. "None of what I've learned prepared me for *you.*"

Emily giggled again, then covered her mouth with both hands.

"Go tell Aden we'll be along in a few minutes," Ethan said to her.

"You sound certain I'll be coming with you," Russ said slowly.

Ethan spread his hands. "Aren't you at all curious about us? I'm giving you a chance to see how we live; to decide for yourself--with no lies, no untruths--whether or not we are the monsters you think we are. My house would be open to you. I would hold no secrets."

"Why would you give me that chance if I could turn around and destroy you?" Russ asked.

Ethan took a moment to reply, as if choosing his words with care. "There *are* vampires who make the rest of us look like monsters," he said. "Who prey on humans and kill for their own pleasure. I'll not deny that. And I would agree that those vampires need to be punished. And sometimes, that punishment means death. In those cases, I would welcome a human judge."

Russ couldn't disagree with that. And perhaps Ethan saw something in the expression on his face, or his posture, or something, because he only hesitated a moment before continuing.

"But in all other cases? We live. We pass as humans most of the time. We hold jobs. We pay taxes. We vote. And just because we rely on humankind to live, does that mean the rest of us are monsters, too?"

"I thought so," Russ whispered. "I've always been told that was true."

"Don't you think it's time that you made up your own mind?" Ethan asked.

"A vampire murdered my sister," Russ said. "When I was seventeen." He hadn't meant to tell Ethan anything, but the words slipped out. "His actual target was my sister's friend--she died, too--along with the other two people in the car."

"What happened to the vampire?" Ethan asked quietly.

"I killed him," Russ said. "With a kitchen knife." He tried to smile, but he couldn't dredge up enough strength to make it stick. "A late-blooming talent brought on by stress. My sister's friend came back; I don't know what happened to her."

But he could guess, and so could Ethan.

"I won't say he shouldn't have died," Ethan said. "But your sister's friend? She was an innocent in this."

"What if I don't change my mind?" Russ asked. "What if I decide that you *are* monsters? What then? You call your experiment a failure and kill me anyway?"

"I give you my word that you will leave my care alive and whole," Ethan said. "All I ask in exchange is--"

"My word that I will not harm you or yours," Russ murmured. "You've told me that already." He wiped one hand across his face. Did he have any other choice if he wanted to live? Did he want to live? He knew what would happen if Ethan kept his word; he'd return to the fold and they would debrief him, and isolate him from everyone for months until they were satisfied he wasn't either a vampire or a spy.

But if Ethan kept his word, and allowed him to leave, would he have to go back?

That thought stopped him cold. Why *wouldn't* he go back? He was a Hunter. He had no other skills; no other desire in life than to hunt vampires. If he vanished off the face of the earth, he'd have to look over his shoulder for the rest of his life, because there were *vampires* out there who wanted him dead. If the Hunters claimed him compromised, they'd put a price on his head as well.

Did he have any chance at all to live somewhere quietly with Naomi and Rosemarie? To see his daughter grow up? Vampire Hunters didn't retire; they died. There were no alternatives.

Were there?

Would he have any chance at all if he took Ethan's offer and changed his mind?

Did it matter?

"I have one small request if you don't mind," Russ said slowly.

"Name it," Ethan said.

"Could I...Naomi and I didn't part on good terms," Russ said. "Could I call her? They're likely to tell her I'm dead, and I...I would rather she not grieve for me."

"Hmm." Ethan folded his arms. Stroked his chin. "I think we'd have to ask Niles if he could block any sort of tracking spell they might have on her phone," he said. "But it could be done if he agrees he could do such a thing."

Russ nodded. "Thank you." He felt odd again, short of breath; his fingers tingling, his vision bordered with gray. "Then you have my word."

And there; he had broken almost fifteen years of blind acceptance with a single sentence.

He started to get up; actually made it to his feet before Ethan caught his arm as he swayed.

"You look terrible," the vampire said. "Why don't you lie down for a bit? Aden can wait."

And Russ was so numb that he allowed Ethan to maneuver him across the room to the bed, and he was so numb that he didn't even care that a *vampire* pulled the sheets back the rest of the way and carefully helped him lie down. He was numb enough to close his eyes and allow himself to drift away without stopping to consider the fact that he had given his word to a vampire, and that he meant to keep it.

Chapter 2

He awoke much later to find he'd sprawled out in the bed on his stomach; his back protested when he rolled over, but otherwise, he'd slept like the dead, completely without dreams or portents.

"You snore," Niles said from the paisley chair.

"I've been told that before," Russ replied, and sat on the edge of the bed. "You double-crossed me."

From under his length of bangs, Niles looked vaguely uneasy. He opened his mouth to reply, but Russ waved away his response.

"I would have done the same if I were you."

"I thought you'd be angry," Niles said.

"I gave Ethan my word I wouldn't harm anyone here," Russ replied. "And I don't give my word lightly."

Niles nodded and brushed his bangs away from his eyes. "I'm sorry I had to hit you so hard," he said. "I didn't want anyone to get hurt."

"Apology accepted," Russ said.

"Ethan said you wanted to make a phone call," Niles said, and held out a slim cellphone. "It's warded; it's also prepaid. And the person on the bill lives in Montana."

Russ nodded. "That should throw them off the scent."

"Should? Or will?" Niles asked.

"Well...if I were the one doing the tracing, it would take me a while to pinpoint the deception," Russ said. "I'm not going to say it wouldn't be impossible to trace, but to here? Probably not."

"What would you do differently?" Niles asked.

Russ realized suddenly that he was talking about deceiving some of the same Hunters he'd helped train. Or, in Andre's case, had trained completely. Did it matter? He *didn't* want to be found here, like this.

"Let's see," he said, and opened the phone.

He added another layer of wards on top of Niles' very thorough wards, and then tweaked the phone's electronics to mimic the signal of a different provider entirely. He routed any call through three different cell phone towers in three different states, and set a trap so that if someone *did* get too close, the phone itself would self-destruct. And he was very much aware of Niles' intent regard, watching him befuddle his own trail.

And, no doubt making sure he wasn't adding in something that would make him easier to find.

"Do you see what I did?" he asked.

"Yes," Niles said. "I wouldn't have thought of all of that."

"You might need to someday," Russ replied. "If you're Ethan's only tech wizard--"

Niles stiffened. "And what if I am?"

"Then you need to be aware," Russ said. "And if you're not, then however many of you there are need to work together. May I make my phone call?"

"Of course," Niles said. "I'll wait outside."

Russ dialed Naomi's number, waited for the elaborate smokescreen to fall into place with a series of clicks and quite a bit of static, and finally heard her pick up on the other end.

"Hello?"

She sounded like she had been crying.

"Hello? Who is this?"

Russ cleared his throat. "Naomi?"

Silence on the other end. A shocked indrawn breath, almost a sob.

Russ spoke quickly, trying to get everything out before his courage deserted him. "Naomi, I'm not sure what they told you or if they've been there yet, but I'm alive. I'm fine. I've not been harmed."

"No, no sign of him," Naomi said, and he could tell she was crying now. And he knew, without a doubt, that she wasn't alone. "They've been searching the forest, but they haven't found him yet."

"I don't think I'll be able to call you again," Russ said softly. "Not for a little while, at least. But I wanted to call to tell you that I love you. I love you and Rosemarie. And I don't want to give you up."

Naomi laughed through her tears. "The funny thing is, when he left I told him I never wanted to see him again. But now? Now all I want to do is tell him I love him. And I hope he comes home soon."

"Don't tell them I called you," Russ said. "Please don't tell them. They won't be able to trace this call."

To someone else, Naomi said, "It's my friend Laura, from Scotland. I emailed her last night."

Scotland? Oh. Andre's last name was Dunfaddin.

"I have no idea why it's not coming up on your screen," Naomi said, and Russ could hear annoyance in her voice now. "It's an overseas call. Maybe your technology isn't as good as you think it is."

"It's good, but I'm better," Russ said when she came back to the phone. "Do you know if they found anything? My van? My paperwork?"

"Not a thing," Naomi said, and he heard anger in her voice now. Not towards him; towards the Hunters, who had no doubt set up shop in her parents' formal dining room, or worse. "They haven't even been able to find his last known whereabouts. All *I* know is that he was somewhere in Kentucky."

A voice spoke in the background; a *familiar* voice. Andre. And Naomi spoke, stiffly, "You'll take this phone from my cold dead hand!"

"I'm alive," Russ said. "I intend to remain that way. Don't tell them I called. I'll call you again as soon as I can. I love you, Naomi."

"I'll let you know as soon as I find out anything," Naomi said softly. "Thanks for calling." She paused, and then whispered, "Love you, too."

There was a scuffle, then, and Russ heard Andre's voice, far too close. And then the phone disconnected; someone had ended the call. Russ closed the phone he held in his hand and sat on the edge of the bed, staring at the wall, struggling with the storm of emotion that threatened to spill over into something best left alone.

Andre would not give up looking for him. Russ had trained him well.

Russ stood, pocketed the phone, and walked to the door. When he opened it, he wasn't surprised to find Ethan waiting there with Niles. "How thoroughly did you hide my van?"

"It's in the garage," Ethan said. "Behind the house wards. We thought since *you* couldn't penetrate them--"

"Not good enough," Russ said. "Andre won't give up. He'll find a way to track it here. I left a paper trail, after all; I've bought gas, and food--"

"Wood for stakes," Ethan commented.

Russ folded his arms. "Yes. That, too. Do you want him to find me here or not? He won't come alone; he'll bring an army of Hunters with him. It's entirely up to you."

"What do you need us to do?" Niles asked.

"*I'm* going to have to do it," Russ replied. He smiled at the expression on Ethan's face. "I gave you my word."

"And I told you I wouldn't hide anything from you," Ethan said. "But...the *wards?*"

"It would have taken me a day or two longer to get past them," Russ said. "They're good, but I'm better." He said this without a single ounce of boasting.

"Well, he *did* cloak the cell phone in so many layers that you could probably call the head Hunter right now and they wouldn't have a chance of tracing the call," Niles said into the silence.

"However tempting that would be, I think I'll decline," Ethan said, still staring at Russ.

"There is no middle ground," Russ said. "Either let me in or let me leave. I gave you my word. If the Hunters find you here because of me, I'll have broken it. And when I give my word--"

"Oh, let him do it, Ethan," a voice said from the end of the hall. "It certainly couldn't hurt."

It was a crotchety old voice that belonged to an equally old woman who stood with Emily beside her, leaning heavily on a twisted wooden cane. A *human* woman, although there was something a bit odd about her. A wizard, definitely; Russ recognized her touch in the wards around the house.

"I sent Aden home," the woman said. "And decided to come myself." She smiled. "It's not every day you get to see a live Hunter."

"You don't see dead ones often either," Russ said.

The old woman laughed. "True. Although I've seen quite a few in my time." She walked as if the cane was an annoyance; slamming it against the floor with every step. Russ wondered if she'd ever caught someone's foot with it. Emily seemed well-aware of its reach. "Russell Moore. I've heard a lot about you. Almost all of it is bad. But that, of course, is from *our* perspective, not yours."

"You know *my* name; what is yours?" Russ asked.

"Dahlia Walker," the woman said, and laughed anew at the expression on his face. "I'm not quite as dead as you lot thought. They call me 'grandmother' around here; I can't imagine why. Although the young ones call me Dolly. *You* can call me Ms. Walker."

"And what do *you* think of Ethan's quest for peace?" Russ asked.

The old woman snorted. "It's about time something is done about this travesty of a 'war'. It's gone on way past the time it should have ended. I'm not sure Ethan's approach is the best way, but you're standing here talking to us, aren't you?"

"With your permission, then?" Russ asked, and Ethan finally nodded.

It felt odd to stand on the other side of a vampire's wards and not try to tear them down. And they *were* good wards. But from this side, he found the flaw, or a small series of them; nothing someone would see while looking at the whole, but something that didn't work with something else without a patch that no one had created.

Until now.

"Maybe if you change your mind, you could do wards for a living," Niles said, and Russ noticed that while Ethan had lost track of his movements some time ago, Niles had no trouble keeping up.

"Maybe," Russ agreed, and released them back to where they belonged. "Ms. Walker?"

The old woman had closed her eyes about halfway through. But now, she opened them and nodded to Russ. "You have a good mind," she said. "It's a shame you've wasted it on the Hunters."

"Grandmother--" Ethan began.

She waved him away. "You are lucky he keeps his word," she said. "Otherwise, I'd be afraid we'd all be dead in our beds by tomorrow night."

"By tomorrow night?" Russ asked. "Why then?"

"You don't know where you are, and you don't know the layout of this house," Dahlia Walker said. "You might have discerned some of that from the wards--"

"I know there's no one else here but us," Russ replied. "So Ethan didn't lie to me when he said this wasn't his house."

"But the wards encompass everything," Ethan said. "And I *do* own this house."

"Okay, then," Russ said. "There are two other buildings inside the wards. But there are secondary wards on one of the buildings; I didn't touch those. If a Hunter managed to get past what I did to your wards, then they can damn well get caught in the secondaries."

Ethan smiled. "Thank you."

"They'll still find my paper trail," Russ said. "I can't do anything about that."

"We'll have to take that risk," Ethan said. "I know you weren't staying anywhere--"

"I usually sleep in my van."

Niles opened his mouth, as if he wanted to comment on that, but he closed his mouth when Dahlia Walker spoke.

"Now that we've got that settled, are we going to stand here and chat, or are you going to introduce him to the others?" she asked.

Ethan hesitated. Dahlia snorted. "You can't back out now."

"I have no intention of backing out," Ethan said, almost sharply. "I, too, gave my word."

"Then what are you waiting for?" Emily asked, speaking up for the first time.

Russ thought he knew, but he held his tongue. Keeping him here, in an empty house was one thing. Actually allowing him to venture into his home...he didn't blame Ethan for his caution.

"Nothing at all," Ethan finally said. "Mr. Moore might want to change his clothes before he meets the others."

"There are clothes in my van," Russ said, because he *had* worn the same clothes for days now, and he hadn't taken a shower since the last time he'd stopped at a motel for the night. "If you don't mind waiting--"

Dahlia shot Ethan a look that was part annoyance, part exasperation. "We'll wait."

Niles left, then, and returned a few minutes later with a selection of clothing, including Russ' jacket with its hidden pockets--and the tiny vials of garlic-laced olive oil he'd never had to use.

As a peace offering, he said, "You might want to empty the jacket before you give it to me to wear." And then, before they could reply, he left them to unzip the pockets and carried the rest of the clothes into the bathroom.

Fifteen minutes later, he was cleaner, and Niles had amassed a pile of easily hidden weaponry on the bedside table. Vials of oil, silver dust; it was a lifetime's collection, and Ethan was a bit paler than normal. Even Dahlia seemed a bit taken aback.

"It's like housing a nuclear weapon in the garage," he murmured when Russ stepped out into the bedroom.

"I'm very good at my job," Russ said, and it was almost an apology. "If you'd rather not go through with this, I'll understand."

"No," Ethan said, slowly. "I said I would open my house to you. And I will do that."

Niles did something with the weaponry; for all Russ knew, he flushed it down the toilet, although what broken glass would do to the septic system, Russ didn't want to know. But the pile vanished, and Russ put on his jacket, now much lighter, and with Ethan leading, they walked outside.

It was early evening; the sun had set, but the sky was still light enough to see that this house was the one Russ had been watching; he'd seen pictures on the county auditor's website and they weren't that different than the truth. But the other house; farther back in the woods, and the other building which could have been a garage of some sort, were not on the property records at all.

"I hope we're driving," Dahlia said.

"Yes." Ethan's voice was soft, remote.

"The others are waiting for us to arrive," Emily said, and Ethan blinked, then glanced at Russ.

"I should warn you," he said. "There are some who do not agree with my decision to bring you here."

"That's no surprise," Russ said. "What are you trying to tell me?"

Ethan shook his head. "I think it would have been better if Aden had stayed," he said, evidently to himself.

"Ethan," Dahlia snapped. And then, to Russ, she said, "Your presence here makes everyone nervous. Just--remember you gave your word."

"And if I have to defend myself?" Russ asked. "What then?"

"Try not to kill anyone," Niles murmured under his breath.

"Let's just hope it doesn't come to that," Ethan said, and smiled a smile so fake Russ half-expected it to crack and fall away. "Follow me."

A vampire's car was not unlike anyone else's car, although the active wards were impressive enough for Russ to take notice. His hands itched to examine them, but he kept his talent tightly controlled.

Dahlia sat up front with Ethan, she claimed age before necessity and Ethan made no protest. Russ found himself in the backseat with Niles and Emily, the latter who perched in the middle with a grin on her face, as if sitting next to a Hunter was a special treat.

It was a silent car ride down a winding gravel road; a mile into the forest, maybe a bit more. Russ desperately wanted to read the secondary wards to see what was waiting for him, but he had no time to prepare. Even though Ethan drove slowly, the house loomed up ahead only a couple minutes later.

And there was, of course, a welcoming committee standing silently in front of an open garage door; five vampires and two humans. At first, Russ thought that one of the humans was sitting in a chair, but then the car's headlights illuminated the wheels and he realized that the man sat in a wheelchair with a blanket over his legs.

Ethan stopped the car because they were standing in front of the garage door; after a moment of conversation, the group moved away so he could pull the car into the garage. Russ watched them as they passed. He sensed no malice from them, but they didn't look very happy.

"You twitch when you're nervous," Niles said, amused, and Russ realized he'd been drumming his fingers on his knees since the house had appeared.

"The man in the wheelchair is Aden?" he asked.

"Yes," Ethan said shortly.

"Then this might not be a good idea after all," Russ said, remembering a night, long ago, and what had happened to his partner at the time, at the hands of one particular wizard intent on protecting a house full of vampires.

And what he had done to the man before his own wounds had overcome him; he'd awakened in the hospital, hooked up to tubes and machines.

His partner had died. Russ had always assumed that the wizard had died, too.

"Wait one second," Dahlia said, and twisted around to face him. "You *know* Aden?"

"Ten years ago, he wasn't in that wheelchair," Russ said. He could hardly force the words from between numb lips. He heard the door open beside him; braced himself for a blow, or an attack, or *something,* but instead he heard a voice.

"And there are wounded in every war," Aden said, and Russ glanced at him, avoiding the chair; looking at his face, no longer as young, but still familiar. He moved a lever on the chair's arm, and it slid smoothly backwards. "Why do you think I gave your name to Ethan?"

"You didn't tell *me* that," Ethan said, and Russ heard a current of anger running through his words.

"Would you have agreed to this if I had told you?" Aden asked.

"No," Ethan said. "Probably not."

"And your noble dream would still be a dream and nothing more," Aden said softly. To Russ, he said, "Come in. Meet the others." A smile flew across his lips. "They won't bite."

Ethan laughed. Dahlia snorted. Emily giggled, and even Niles hid a smile.

Russ couldn't reply to that. He nodded to Aden, slid out of his seat and stood there while Emily clambered out and threw her arms around Aden's neck.

"Ride me?" she begged.

"Climb aboard," Aden said, and led the way into the house.

Russ felt as if he was walking to his death, even though no one had treated him with anything but respect. The whole situation; walking into a vampire's house without a single weapon save for his talents felt so strange that he kept trying to convince himself that this was a dream and nothing more. He walked behind Ethan, with Dahlia at his back, thumping away. The tension couldn't have been more exquisitely painful if Dahlia had transformed her cane into a sword and stabbed him in the back.

And then, when Aden stopped at a closed door, almost as if someone had prompted her, Emily slid off his lap and solemnly stopped beside Russ. And held out her hand.

And Russ took it; took her offering, and suddenly, he didn't feel so alone anymore.

Aden opened the door and vanished inside. Ethan followed him. And after a moment, Emily tugged on his hand.

"Come on," she said.

Dahlia poked him in the back with her cane. "I'm not going to wait all night long, young man."

And Russ stepped forward...into silence.

There were about twenty vampires in the room, and ten humans, but that only counted the adults. The children were safely corralled in their parents' arms--in one case, a teenaged vampire held what seemed to be her little sister--and three of the vampires who had waited outside with Aden clustered together near an open door.

Emily pointed to a woman who sat near the teenaged vampire. "That's my Mommy."

"Then I have her to thank for breakfast," Russ said, and the woman smiled, and rose, and approached him with her hand outstretched.

"I'm Nadine Walker," she said. "Welcome to our home."

Her gesture seemed to break some thread of tension, because someone else approached, and then someone else, and then the whole clan seemed to converge on him, human and vampire alike. Emily stuck by his side, self-appointing herself as his protector; she frowned at the ones who offered him veiled insults--that he ignored--and smiled at the ones who seemed genuinely pleased to meet him.

The three vampires near the door did not move until their fourth had arrived, and by then, Aden had noticed their reluctance and he had already wheeled himself over to where they stood. And they spoke; Aden motioned towards Russ and one of the vampires made a rude gesture, and--

"Don't pay attention to them," Ethan said from beside him.

"And have them attempt a coup while I'm here?" Russ asked. "Or try to murder me in my bed?"

"They wouldn't dare," Ethan said shortly. "And Emily, your mother says it's time to go to bed."

Emily started to pout, but a yawn ruined her effort and she rubbed her eyes. "I'm not tired."

"Yes, you are," Ethan said. "Go to sleep. He'll still be here in the morning."

Emily glanced at Russ. "I'll still be here in the morning," he agreed, and she nodded, yawned again, and tottered off to where her mother waited.

The room slowly emptied out. Those with children left first; the others lingered for a little while longer, but long before dawn, Aden, Ethan, and Russ were the only ones left in the room. Even Dahlia had left, muttering something about being too old to stay up all night.

"Where's Niles?" Russ asked, because he'd noticed his absence some time before. Had he been in the procession from the car to this room? Russ couldn't remember.

"He's eliminating any sign of your presence from the other house," Ethan said. "You'll be staying here now."

Russ nodded. For a moment--a very *short* moment--he had forgotten that he was, in effect, a prisoner, despite the way they had welcomed him. He'd forgotten that Ethan and the others were supposed to be the enemy. He'd *forgotten.*

He caught the tail end of Ethan's smile as he turned away, and realized that the vampire knew exactly what had passed through Russ' mind. Which was the point, of course, of keeping him here. Wasn't there a term for that? When the hostage started to sympathize with the kidnapper's point of view?

"It's late," Aden said, interrupting his train of thought. "I'll show you to your room if you'd like."

Russ opened his mouth to, potentially, say something he'd regret later, but found himself nodding instead. "Thank you."

He would have to sort out the emotional aspects of everything later.

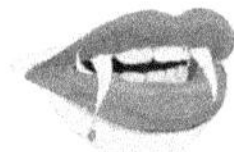

The room Aden led him to was plainly, but comfortably, furnished. A bed, a small table, a lamp, a bookcase full of what looked to be historical fiction. The clothes he'd changed out of lay folded on the bed, freshly laundered. There was a phone on the bedside table, too. Russ stared at it for a moment, then turned to Aden with a question on his lips that died when he saw the expression on Aden's face.

"He's putting everyone's life on the line by trusting you," Aden said fiercely.

"I know," Russ said. "I gave him my word. I intend to keep it." He backed up as Aden advanced into the room, well-aware that he walked a fine line with this; if Aden had been the one behind Ethan's experiment in the first place, then alienating him was not a good idea at all.

"Will your word hold your training in check if you are attacked?" Aden asked, and Russ sat down on the bed to face him.

"I don't know," he said. "I would hope so. But I can't--" He stood up and walked over to the window. Opened the curtain to peek out at the darkened forest. "I almost wish I *was* helpless. It would be easier."

"So it would be harder for you to restrain yourself from murdering us all?" Aden asked, slightly mocking.

"No," Russ said. "So it would be harder for me to react if someone were to overreact to something I said, or did. Because if I defend myself, who will be the villain?"

"You don't think this will work, do you?" Aden asked.

Russ remembered his feeling just moments before. And he almost didn't mention it; he almost didn't say anything about it at all. "What I told Ethan earlier is true. I'm already compromised. The Hunters won't believe I wasn't enchanted, or worse. If I return to them or if they find me, I'll spend the next few months locked away from everyone while they decide if I they can ever trust me again." He hesitated. Plunged on. "And I'm not sure they *could* ever trust me again."

"What?" Aden moved closer, the whir of the wheelchair's mechanisms loud in Russ' ears. "What did you say?"

"Right before we left that room; right before we came here, I felt as if I were a guest in this house," Russ whispered. "Not a prisoner. A *guest*." He folded his arms and leaned against the wall. "For a moment, I forgot who I was. Who I'm supposed to be. What I've been trained to do."

Aden was silent for a long moment, staring at him. And then, still silent, he turned and left the room, closing the door behind him.

Closing it. Not locking it. Trusting him. Russ sank down in the chair. Put his head in his hands. Tried not to think about what that meant, or Aden's silence.

After a little while, he turned on the tiny television on the other side of the room, just for the sake of human company and nothing more. He had no idea how many shows he sat through, staring at the flickering display without really seeing it at all before he roused himself enough to pick up the phone.

There was a dial tone. And no wards, save for the ones that surrounded the house.

Russ desperately wanted to talk to someone; someone neutral; to ask someone if Ethan was right and he was wrong. He needed a second opinion, but he had no one to call. He *had* no outside friends. No one had ever tried to give him the argument that vampires weren't merciless killers.

No one had ever given him the chance to find out.

He didn't remember each and every vampire he had killed; he *couldn't* remember that without going mad. But their faces haunted him; their pleading haunted him; he couldn't escape the whispers in his head.

He hung up the phone. He was alone in this. Utterly alone. Whatever decision he made would haunt him for the rest of his life. Either that, or kill him, depending on the outcome.

He closed his eyes. Drifted for a while, then heard the door open; heard the whir of Aden's wheelchair as he ventured into the room.

"Are you asleep?" Aden's voice was soft, uncertain.

"I am too tired to sleep," Russ said, and opened his eyes. "What do you want?"

"Will you show me what you did with the wards?" Aden asked. "Ethan said you did something, but--"

"Niles knows what I did," Russ said. "He watched every move I made. You could ask him; he'll tell you that I didn't--"

"No." Aden shook his head. "It's not that. It's just...I would prefer to know, and Niles isn't back yet."

"Should that be a cause for concern?" Russ asked, awake now, hearing some undercurrents in Aden's voice that he didn't quite understand.

"I'd go ask him myself, but this chair doesn't go very fast on gravel," Aden said.

"How did you get back here before?" Russ asked.

"Righteous indignation, I guess," Aden said. "And a fresh battery. Which is not so fresh at the moment. I have a manual chair for those times in between, but that's almost half a mile."

"I'll show you," Russ said. "But how good are you at wards? Ethan..." Was there a polite way to say it? "Niles had no problem following what I did, but--"

"Ethan's not very good at wards," Aden said, and smiled. "I know. He knows, too. And I realized Dahlia was there as well, but I'm not going to wake her up to ask."

"She might not appreciate that," Russ said, and yawned. "Is there anywhere in this house to get a cup of coffee? A *real* cup of coffee?"

"I heard about the coffee teabags," Aden said, and his smile widened into an actual grin. "Follow me. We can talk more in the kitchen. There's a real, honest-to-goodness coffeemaker there."

"And coffee?" Russ asked.

"There's some in the freezer," Aden said. "They keep it for guests. Vampires, almost as a rule, drink tea."

"Now that would be an interesting research project," Russ said, and followed Aden down the hall. "Healers only drink tea, too. I've never been able to understand it."

"I thought vampire hunters didn't like Healers," Aden said.

Hunters didn't like Healers because Healers didn't discriminate in their choice of patients. But they also knew that Healers couldn't turn anyone away, and despite the hypocrisy, the Hunters had no trouble calling Healers for special circumstances.

"I...I was healed by a Healer once," Russ said, awkward because it had been the same battle in which Aden had lost the use of his legs. "After...after my partner died."

"Oh," Aden said. "I see."

"I'm sorry," Russ whispered, and stopped walking. "Maybe I *shouldn't* be here. Maybe--"

Aden spun his chair around. "Maybe you *shouldn't* be here," he said. "But you are. What you decide to do with that is entirely up to you."

He spoke the truth. And Russ couldn't argue with that.

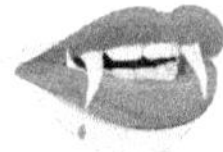

An hour later, they were still in the kitchen and still talking, Russ drinking his third cup of coffee, Aden sticking to tea. Niles wandered in around five o'clock in the morning, only perking up when Russ offered him a cup.

"I wondered what I smelled when I walked in the door," Niles said through a yawn. "What are you doing?"

"Talking," Aden said. "About wards."

"Why aren't you asleep like every other person in this house?"

"I needed coffee," Russ said.

"And I wanted information," Aden replied.

Niles shook his head. "I'm sure that's a fascinating conversation, but I'm going to bed. Don't wake me up unless it's a dire emergency."

"What constitutes a dire emergency around here?" Russ asked, only half-joking.

Niles stopped in the doorway. "Fire?" he suggested. "Floods? Hunters?" He peered at Russ, bleary-eyed, but astute enough to notice something Russ couldn't quite pinpoint himself. "You're--"

"Go to bed," Aden said. "We'll be headed that way soon."

Niles frowned, but did his bidding and vanished down the hall.

"I think I can sleep now," Russ said, and finished off the coffee.

"I'm not sure how, considering how much of that stuff you've had," Aden replied, and yawned. "Sleep sounds good."

Russ pinched the bridge of his nose. "Very good, in fact."

Aden accompanied him back to his room. Russ didn't even turn on the light. He fell into bed, fully clothed, and slept too soundly for dreams.

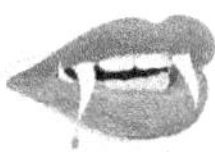

A week passed, then two. Ethan came and went, Emily stuck by his side when he was awake, and Aden or Niles were never far away. There were no attacks in the night; no coups, no rebellion against Russ' presence. In fact, Russ didn't see the group of young vampires again. He decided not to ask if they had been sent away.

He lost track of time. He remembered names of the faces he'd seen that first night, and they went out of their way to be accommodating, to welcome him.

Safe and secure within a vampire's home, Russ slept soundly for the first time in years. And he realized, early on, that he would not be able to go back.

The breaking point came when a small group of vampires showed up at Ethan's door one night, victims of Hunters the next county over. Four vampires, one human--all wounded--and a baby; Russ was closest to the mother when she started to fall, and was the only one close enough to catch the child--a vampire--before he tumbled to the floor.

And after that, after staunching wounds and cradling the baby when he cried; after watching one of the vampires succumb to silver poisoning and watching the others pull through, he realized that Ethan's experiment had worked. He could not go back now. And he realized that he missed his own family--he missed both Naomi and Rosemarie--more than he missed the Hunters who had nurtured him for so long.

He wasn't really surprised when Dahlia appeared outside his door three days after the group of vampires arrived.

"It's time for you to go, isn't it?" she asked.

"Yes, I think so," Russ said, and put his finger to his lips because he was on baby duty since Jeffrey's mother was still in the infirmary, recovering. "My daughter's first birthday is in two weeks. I'd like to see her again." He'd lost track of time, but not the date; the days had marched onward with distressing regularity.

"I think it would be best if you all made a new start," Dahlia said. "We could help with that."

"A new start?" Russ asked.

"In a different town," Dahlia said. "Not unlike the way the vampires start over when the Hunters get wind of their presence."

Russ had called Naomi only one other time. And she'd told him of the Hunters' desperate--and fruitless--search for any sign of him; and how Andre had grown so suspicious of everyone that she'd finally kicked him out of the house and thrown all of his stuff out with him.

What would she say if he told her she'd have to abandon everything and go into hiding if she wanted to stay with him?

"I don't think she'd agree to that," Russ said. "But I'll ask her."

"She may need to if she wants to stay with you," Dahlia said.

Russ nodded. "I know." He hesitated. "I'm not the kind of person to stay silent on the sidelines for long, you realize."

"I know you're not," Dahlia said. "But...what can one person do against the Hunters?"

"I could have tried my best to ensure Jeffrey didn't lose his father four days ago," Russ said softly.

"And if your daughter loses hers?" Dahlia asked. "What then?"

"She'll know I wasn't a bad person," Russ said. "She'll know I was trying to make amends."

"Making amends is not a requirement of this," Dahlia said. "That wasn't Ethan's intention--"

"I know," Russ said.

"You'd put your family in danger--"

"They're already in danger." Which was true, and even Dahlia couldn't argue with that. "If I can get Naomi to agree to move; to go into hiding, then we can make a life for ourselves that way. But I can't...I *won't* sit on the sidelines and watch this continue."

"We did not ask for that," Dahlia said, as if bound and determined to talk him out of it.

"Who else will do it?" Russ countered. "Of course, I'd appreciate it if you...spread the word a bit; I don't think I'll be welcome in many places otherwise."

Dahlia smiled. "I think we could do that."

"Thank you, Ms. Walker," Russ said.

"I think, considering the circumstances, you can call me Dolly," Dahlia Walker replied, and walked away.

There were plans to be made, of course. Phone calls to make, to Naomi, only one argument when she realized what he intended to do. Careful wards to set, and deceptions, distractions; it was the hardest subterfuge Russ had ever crafted.

Naomi was to pack one bag for herself and the baby, and meet Niles at the bus station. From there, Niles was to take them to the nearest city where Russ would be waiting. And Russ would spirit them away.

That was the plan, at least. Simple, yet complicated in its design. There were so many spells in place; so many layers that Russ *knew* he had missed something. Complications, in wards and spells, were never good things at all.

And so he paced, and checked the smokescreens and the wards over and over again. Examining them for any sign of weakness. Finding nothing. He spoke on the phone with Naomi twice more; she spoke of the Hunters, still searching for him. She didn't quite believe they were just letting him go. He assured her all was well.

And then there was Andre, who had followed her home from the grocery store one night. And little things, inside the house, misplaced things. Naomi's cell phone vanished for an hour and reappeared in a space she'd searched twice.

After that, Russ had her buy a prepaid phone. *That* particular paper trail could not be helped.

And then, after days of waiting, it was time. The first part of the plan went off without a hitch. The second--

It was Niles' phone call that alerted Russ that something was wrong.

"She's not here," Niles said, his voice tinny and small through a bad connection and the speakerphone in the kitchen. "She's not here, but there are Hunters here."

Russ had dialed Naomi's new number almost before Niles stopped speaking. It rang and rang and rang and rang before someone picked up--and that someone was not Naomi.

"Hello, Russ." Andre's voice was as smooth as ever.

Russ couldn't move, or speak. He dropped the phone; Ethan caught it and held it out to him, his gaze anguished.

"Andre," Russ whispered.

"By now, of course, you've probably realized that Naomi's not going to meet whoever it is you sent to the bus station," Andre said as if they were talking about the weather.

"Why not?" Russ' face was frozen; his lips numb. Someone's hand was on his arm, coaxing him into a chair; he resisted, but only momentarily. It was either sit or fall down, and he didn't want to fall. Not now.

"She lied to me," Andre said, still conversationally, still friendly. "Do you know what happens to people who lie to vampire hunters?"

"Niles, get out of there," Ethan said in a whisper. Not loud enough for Andre to hear. "Get out of there *now.*"

"I'm gone," Niles said.

Russ barely heard him. "What did you do to them?" He couldn't force his voice above a whisper.

"*You* trained me," Andre said, and laughed. "What do you *think* I did to them?"

A yawning chasm of blackness opened up inside Russ' mind. He couldn't think past the panic; couldn't breathe; couldn't move.

"Why don't you come here and find out?" Andre continued when he didn't reply. "I promise I won't kill you."

A vampire hunter's promise could not be trusted. Russ struggled past the numbness. "Andre, she is just a little baby--"

"Ah, but she was *your* little baby," Andre said, and Russ' mind fastened on the word 'was'. "And a baby can't live long without its mother."

"Andre--"

"Come to the house, Russ," Andre said. "See for yourself." And before Russ could reply to that, he hung up the phone.

Automatically, Russ dialed the number again. This time, it went into voicemail and he heard Naomi's voice urging him to leave a message.

Ethan was still talking to Niles; Aden looked sickened, as if he had heard some of the conversation. Dahlia's mouth was set into a thin line.

"You can't go," Emily said, and Russ hadn't even realized she was in the room. He turned to stare at her; she stepped back away from him, her eyes too bright. Had she heard--?

"I have to," Russ said simply.

"You can't," Ethan said. "It's a trap; he wants to draw you out. I'm sure they're fine--"

"He said 'was'," Emily whispered, stricken. "He said *was*, not 'is'."

"I know," Russ said, still numb. "I have to go. Now. And none of you can go with me."

"Call as soon as you get there," Aden said, and now he was frustrated; frustrated and angry. "Or else we *will* come after you."

"I'll drive you to your van," Ethan said, and it was the shortest half mile ride Russ had ever been on; in silence, with a vampire beside him. Emily had hugged him, crying; Dahlia had started to speak, but had swallowed her words.

He hadn't driven the van in a month; hadn't started it in that long, but it started right up--for him, of course it did--and he drove. He drove as fast as he could possibly drive, swerving in and out of traffic, keenly aware that either the cops or the Hunters could pull him over at any time.

But--hours later, almost dawn--he made it to the little white house. Just a small frame house, nothing special; nothing remarkable, other than the fact that his family lived there; his daughter and his wife, both of whom were probably dead.

Every light in the house was burning, casting shadows on the lawn. The neighbors weren't close enough for anyone to notice yet. Russ exited the van almost before it had stopped and left the driver's door open; he didn't care anymore, what would happen if Andre got past his wards.

He only cared about Naomi and Rosemarie.

The front door was open, only an inch, but a line of light spilled from the crack; a line of candlelight, not lamplight. Andre could have easily killed him right there and then as he hesitated at the door, but he didn't. Nothing happened. To every inch of Russ' senses, the house was empty.

Then why did he smell blood?

He pushed open the door. The candlelight flickered in the wind of his passage; hundreds of candles, burning on every available surface, using every available plate and bowl and saucer as holders. A few of the candles had guttered out; most were still burning. Russ ignored them and moved farther into the house. Walked down the pathway Andre had left him and tried not to smell the blood.

Past the hallway, into the kitchen. There was a knife missing from the block, but the kitchen itself seemed no different than the last time he'd been there. No blood here.

He moved on.

One of the dining room chairs lay on its side. Russ straightened it absently, and saw a single drop of blood on the carpet--still tacky when he touched it. But cold. Cold like his heart, his mind, his soul.

There were three bedrooms in the house. Two upstairs, one downstairs. The downstairs bedroom's door was closed. The bathroom door was closed as well. Russ opened the bathroom door first. It was empty of bodies, but it was not empty of blood. He found a hand towel on the toilet, just sitting there, used, with streaks of blood staining the white cotton, and his heart clenched.

He turned around. Crossed the short space of hallway. Opened the other door.

Stopped with his hand on the light switch, because this light wasn't on. Or perhaps the bulb had burned out; perhaps Andre had intended for him to see them clearly when he first opened the door.

There were shapes in the bed. He could see that much.

Through tears, methodically, he walked into the room and turned on the bedside lamp.

They lay together, mother and daughter, arranged as if Rosemarie had fallen asleep on Naomi's chest. Save for the blood drenching their clothes and the paleness of their skin, they looked like they were sleeping.

Russ looked for the knife, but he didn't find it. He reached out, one hand hovering over his baby daughter's little head; the soft wisps of hair; the rosebud lips.

He let his hand drop. He couldn't help them now. He had failed.

The cell phone rang in his pocket. Russ ignored it. When it beeped, he took it out of his pocket and tossed it at the wall. He sat down beside the bed and took Naomi's hand; curled Rosemarie's little fingers around his own. And in the end, he held them; his family, shattered now, forever, and he sobbed.

Vampire hunters had two rules. The second rule, once broken, could never be repaired.

He didn't remember turning out the lights, but he must have, because they were off when he next opened his eyes. He didn't remember covering Naomi and Rosemarie with a white sheet; he *certainly* didn't remember pulling his van into the garage. He couldn't remember when he decided to join his family, but he remembered the acid tang of gasoline when he tried to siphon some out of the gas tank and ended up vomiting on the floor.

He still couldn't find the knife, but really, any knife would do. So he stumbled into the kitchen--when had the sun risen?--and much later--had he passed out on the floor?--he opened his eyes to find a knife in his hand.

It was dark outside again. Sunset had come and gone. Russ' eyes felt as if someone had doused them with sand; he couldn't focus on the clock to see what time it was; to see how long it would be until dawn.

There was only one candle left, burning fitfully in a saucer. Russ sat down on the couch with his knife and watched the candle burn. When it died, then so would he.

He didn't notice when they came inside; he heard Dahlia's cane knock over a candle and its holder first. Niles stepped on one; Russ heard him curse under his breath.

"The van's in the garage," someone else whispered. And then, louder, "Russ?"

A shape moved through the kitchen doorway. Another shape emerged from the hall. Russ kept his gaze fixed on the candle, still barely flickering, still hanging onto life.

And then, Ethan's voice. Urgent. "Bring me a candle, quick!"

"What?" Niles clearly did not understand.

"A candle. I want a candle. *Now.*"

A spit of useless flame. A sputter. A thin thread of smoke, rising from the saucer. The barest hint of an ember, winking. Winking...out.

Russ closed his eyes. Smelled the acrid stench of a lit match. Heard a flame catch.

"Russell?"

He opened his eyes, confused, at first, because there was still one candle lit, still one candle burning strong. And the knife wasn't in his hand anymore, either. His hands were empty. Stained with blood, but empty.

He stared at them. Empty.

Someone flipped on a light in the other room. Russ flinched away from the brightness and fell sideways and almost off the couch. Someone caught him. He tried to struggle.

"Hush, hush," Dahlia said. "Oh, you poor child."

Niles walked into the hallway from the bedroom, his face white. He started to speak; Dahlia hushed him, too.

"This is my fault," he heard Ethan say. "If I hadn't--"

"But you did," Dahlia snapped. "And this is the outcome. The one who did this should be hunted down like the murderer he is and..."

Murderer, Russ' mind commented. *They never did tell you who the murderer was.*

"Who killed Amanda Peabody?" he heard himself ask, his voice a cracked whisper.

"His name is Arthur Dickens," Ethan said after a moment. "I'll tell you exactly where he lives and where to find him if you..."

Russ raised his head. Opened his eyes. Saw that the candle was still burning. "If I what?"

Dahlia released him. Niles still stood in the hallway. Ethan was standing beside the couch, clearly upset. Pacing. Crockery crunched under his feet.

"Look," Ethan said, his voice soft. "If you want to die; if you want to be with them, I will help you die."

"Ethan!" Niles said, shocked.

Ethan ignored him. "I'll take care of Arthur, too. If that will ease your mind."

"Quite a tall order," Dahlia murmured, but Ethan ignored her as well.

"This is not your fault," Russ said, his voice equally soft. "You could not have foreseen this any more than I could have foreseen this." Although-- *should* he have known? He'd *trained* Andre, after all.

His mind was waking up. Remembering. And he wasn't sure he wanted his mind to wake up at all.

He hunched over on the couch and put both hands over his face. Blocking out the sight of the candle. Trying to block out everything else.

He heard Niles whisper a question. Heard Dahlia hush him--again.

"You were intending to kill yourself," Ethan said. "But--"

"I was intending to burn down the house, but I couldn't manage to siphon any gasoline from my van's tank," Russ whispered. He pressed the palms of his hands against his eyes. Lowered his hands. Stared at Ethan, almost challenging. "But what?"

"Another house of vampires was attacked last night," Ethan said quietly. "They're all dead."

"Last night...the night I came here?" Russ asked.

"No. You've been here for two days," Ethan said. "We intended to come to find you sooner, but when we heard about the attack--" his voice trailed away. "There were twenty-five vampires in that household. They are all dead."

"And the humans?" Russ asked, and did not miss the fact that Niles flinched.

"The Hunters locked the humans in the cellar and burned down the house," Ethan said. "We need your help, Russell Moore. We need your *mind.* And your talent." He hesitated. "But if you still wish to die, I will help you."

Dying would mean an end to the heartbreak. Dying would bring him peace.

But living...living, he had a chance to avenge his family's death. And he could thwart the Hunters at every turn. He could make sure someone else's family didn't end up lying cold and dead in someone else's bedroom.

He closed his eyes. Took a deep breath. Felt tears trickle down his cheeks. Absently wiped them away.

"Arthur Dickens first, then," he said, and tried to stand. Almost pitched forward at Ethan's feet.

The vampire helped him up and half-carried him into the kitchen. "Coffee first," he said. "And then some food. And after that, after that, we'll deal with Arthur Dickens."

PART 2

Chapter 1

Ethan called, or contacted a vampire household. Russ would then visit, strengthen their wards with his intimate knowledge of the Hunter's mode of operation, and leave.

Sometimes, afterwards, there was news, mostly good; how the wards had held through a direct attack, or how the vampires had managed to get the upper hand over the Hunters at last.

It was never Andre who was caught, or who died, of course. Andre kept to the shadows, just waiting for the perfect opportunity. But Russ...Russ had a mission.

He was on the road more often than not. In constant motion, sleeping in his van (at least he was used to that). Sometimes, he'd wake up and Niles would be outside, or Ethan, once even Dahlia. They worried about him, he knew that. Ethan felt guilty. Niles tried to engage him in conversation. Dahlia had just sat in silence with him for the evening. Russ insisted--to everyone, and almost believed it himself--that he was fine.

Ethan contacted a vampire household, Russ would visit, strengthen their wards, and then leave...

That was how it was *supposed* to happen, at least.

Until Russ met Ruby.

Ruby was Head of the Tanner Household; among others. A stronghold of vampires that the Hunters had never been able to pierce. A network of smaller houses had formed an alliance under Ruby's house; there were safety in numbers, after all, and their numbers were in the hundreds. They practically owned the whole village, and it wasn't a small village. When Russ drove past the village limits, the wards noted his passing in exacting detail.

He'd been instructed to stop in the village diner for lunch (Ruby-owned) and sit in the booth near the window. His instructions had been detailed down to where he should park his van, and he obeyed them, but only because Ethan had said it would help.

And Russ knew that if Ruby accepted him, if she welcomed him and allowed him to strengthen her wards, then the other vampire households would fall into line for his services. And perhaps--just perhaps--he'd be able to sleep through the night again, something that had never bothered him before.

So he parked his van in the third parking space in front of the diner, got out, locked the door, and walked inside. The only booth in front of the window was empty; the diner had a decent number of patrons for lunch, and the food smelled better than average.

Russ sat. A waitress wearing a green t-shirt, jeans, and a black ball cap brought him a menu, and it actually took him a moment to realize that she was a vampire, and that the wards on the window weren't just for protection against stray Hunters, but sunlight as well.

She smiled at him when she saw he'd figured it out, and vanished into the kitchen. A moment later, she returned with what he'd intended to order--coffee and a BLT doubledecker with french fries.

Russ closed the menu and handed it over. "Thank you. I'll have to admit, I'm impressed." One quick pass of his hand told him the food was safe to eat; she smiled again, but didn't speak, and went to refill drinks at another table.

Fifteen minutes later, she was back, out of uniform, her red hair showing now that she'd taken the ball cap off, but pulled back into a ponytail. She slid into the booth across from him, steepled her hands in front of her face, and said, "Russell Moore."

The BLT had been perfect; the tomatoes fresh, the lettuce crisp, the bacon unburnt. The coffee was just strong enough but not too strong. The French fries were not a soggy mess.

"Yes," Russ said. "And anything you've heard is probably true and I am guilty as charged."

"Then why shouldn't I slay you right here and now and rid the world of a murderer?" she asked, and he had to wonder if *this* was Ruby; the hair fit, but he had no idea what she actually looked like, and neither had Ethan.

"Because I would rather you allow me to live to regret what I did before," Russ said evenly.

"And you want access to my wards so that you can 'strengthen' them," she said, her derision evident.

"You know my name, may I know yours?" Russ asked.

"Ruby Tanner," she said, shortly.

"You're a lot--younger than I expected," Russ said. "Considering you've been head of household for--"

"Sixty-three years," Ruby said. She didn't seem worried that anyone would overhear; Russ had to wonder if the other patrons were members of her family as well. "You follow directions well enough; if I told you to leave and never come back, what would you do?"

"Leave and never come back," Russ said. "Although I was actually eyeing a piece of that lemon meringue pie over there..."

Ruby laughed. "Of course you were," she said, and crooked her finger at someone Russ couldn't see. A moment later, a girl--human--appeared with a piece of lemon meringue pie and a refill for Russ' coffee; he couldn't refuse either one.

Her hair was red as well, and she resembled Ruby quite a bit. "Your daughter?" Russ asked, and the smile fell from Ruby's lips.

"I'm being nice to you because Ethan Walker trusts you and I don't believe he is prone to fancy," Ruby said sharply. "The only reason why I agreed to speak with you was because of Ethan."

"I realize that," Russ said, keeping his voice even. "And I appreciate you allowing me to come. And I realize you don't trust me--" He hadn't checked the pie for poison; now, deliberately, he ate a piece of it and knew she'd noticed immediately. And, no doubt, knew why he had done it.

"You don't seem to be the gambling type," Ruby said after a moment.

"I don't gamble with people's lives," Russ said.

"So when you switched sides--"

"I switched sides," Russ told her. "And although Ethan instigated it, that wasn't the reason why I..."

Ruby's gaze softened. "I heard about your family."

Even now, it was hard to speak of Naomi and Rosemarie without breaking down into tears. But he managed, or tried to. "It wasn't even about them," he said. "While I was Ethan's prisoner, a neighboring family was attacked by Hunters. Only four vampires survived. They came to Ethan's house. I was there when they arrived. There was a little boy, hardly older than my daughter. His name is Jeffrey. His father died that night. His mother almost died. He's going to grow up not knowing his father because of something *I* did."

"But you did not attack them," Ruby said. "You were with Ethan. You had nothing to do with that."

"I was a Hunter," Russ said. "I had *everything* to do with that."

She seemed to realize that he was sincere, at least with this, she studied him for a moment, then nodded, slowly. "You truly believe that you can singlehandedly reverse hundreds of years of Hunter advantage?"

"No, of course not," Russ said. "But I can be a thorn in their sides until they manage to kill me."

"I cannot give you access to my wards," Ruby said. "I have those I answer to, and while my word is law around here, if I ignore their counsel, it won't be *my* word that is law for long."

"I thought there would be resistance," Russ said. "So I'll leave, but I'll leave you with this: Go back to those you answer to and propose a test. The Hunters know of your presence here; they won't sit idle for long. I won't just strengthen your wards. I'll fight them with you."

"You will fight those you helped train," Ruby said, sounding as if she didn't believe him.

"Yes," Russ said, and finished the pie. Drank the coffee. Wondered if it would be out of line to ask for a to-go cup. "And if you have no one talented enough to watch me work, I suggest you ask Ethan to borrow Niles. He's--"

"I have someone talented enough to watch you work," Ruby said, interrupting him. "And I'm afraid the answer will still be no."

"Very well," Russ said. "But the offer still stands, nonetheless." He took out his wallet and pushed his card across the table; Ruby didn't pick it up. But when he pulled out money to pay, she waved it away.

"On the house," she said. "But don't come back."

The wards closed down completely behind him when he drove past the village limits again; he stopped right past the sign and saw what looked to be a police car parked fifty feet away. It followed him out to the highway and twenty miles farther, until it was satisfied he wasn't intending to double back and stir up trouble.

He never drove and used his cell phone at the same time, so he stopped, parked in a fast food restaurant's parking lot, and called Ethan.

"I had a wonderful bacon, lettuce, and tomato sandwich and a piece of lemon meringue pie for lunch, along with some fabulous coffee," Russ said as soon as Ethan picked up.

"But she refused." Ethan didn't really have to guess; Russ suspected he knew she would, at least at first.

"Yes, of course," Russ said. "I gave her my card, but I don't expect a call."

"Where are you now?" Ethan asked.

"In the parking lot of a Chix'n'stix," Russ said. "It must be a local chain; I've never heard of it. I thought I'd stick around for a day or so, just in case she changes her mind--"

"If she calls me I'll let you know," Ethan said. "And I'll try my best to sway her. Any sign of the Hunters?"

"Not as of yet," Russ said. "But the last three times they've attacked, they've failed; they have to be getting desperate for a kill. There are plenty of smaller Houses out there, but--"

"They'll want something big," Ethan said. "Yes. I think so too. Maybe...Maybe I'll call Ruby."

"There's a place where I can park for the night right off the highway about an hour from here," Russ said. "Call if you need to."

"Where will you go next?" Ethan asked.

"I'm not sure," Russ said. "Do you have any other leads for me?"

"Two potentials," Ethan said. "But you've been on the road for eight months straight. Don't you think you should take a break for the summer?"

"Will the Hunters take a break for the summer?" Russ asked.

"I never intended for you to wear yourself down to the bone doing this," Ethan protested.

"I'm fine," Russ said.

"Emily is wondering when you will visit again," Ethan said, and then, as if to prove that he wasn't making that up, Emily's voice came through the phone, loud and clear.

"You've got to come back," she said. "Please?"

Inexplicably, Russ' eyes filled with tears. He didn't speak, but she seemed to sense his distress anyway; she was good at that.

Softer, she said, "We miss you."

"I miss you too," Russ said.

"Aden's been beastly, because he can't drive and no one will take him when they come and visit," Emily said. "And my Mommy won't let me go, either. Will you come back? Just for a little while?"

What would it hurt? Russ knew *why* it would hurt; they would treat him well again, and perhaps he would see pity in their gazes now, because everyone would know what had happened. But he couldn't avoid them forever, could he?

"After I leave here--and I'm staying for a couple more days--I'll come back for a little while," Russ said. "I promise." It would be nice to sleep in a bed again, after all. It would be nice to eat food that wasn't prepared in a restaurant, or on the little hot plate he'd stashed in the back of the van.

"Thank you," Emily said, and he could tell by the tone of her voice that she was smiling. "He said yes!" she crowed, in the background now.

"Don't apologize," Russ said before Ethan could speak.

"Okay, I won't," Ethan said. "I know why you don't want to come back."

"I know you do," Russ said. "But I'm not a coward."

"No, you're not," Ethan told him. "Not at all."

"Let me know if Ruby calls you," Russ said, and Ethan promised to call if she called.

"Be careful," Ethan said. "Ruby is volatile at times, or so I've heard."

"I'm twenty miles away already," Russ said, and started up the van again. "I wasn't anything but polite to her; she has no quarrel with me."

"Even so," Ethan said. "Be careful."

"Goodbye, Ethan," Russ said, amused by his concern, since he'd seen no sign of Hunters, and no one had followed him from Ruby's village once the driver of the police car had been satisfied.

He hung up the phone, placed it on the seat beside him, started the van again, and pulled back onto the road. It was forty minutes to the rest stop he'd seen, public places were the best for safety's sake, and he wouldn't have felt comfortable in a motel. But he also had most of the day to whittle away until dark, so he took the next exit to another little town--this one vampire-free--and spent the afternoon in the local library, a small Carnegie building that had a pretty decent history section, including local interest. And there was even a mention of Ruby's village and of Ruby's diner.

Of course, there were no mentions of vampires.

His phone never rang. Ruby didn't call back to ask him to strengthen her wards, but Russ really hadn't expected her to; he suspected he'd spend the night at the rest stop, then head back to Kentucky the next morning. And perhaps the Hunters would attack Ruby's compound, and perhaps they'd break through her wards. Perhaps they wouldn't. Perhaps he'd get all the way back to Kentucky, only to have her call.

It was late afternoon when he left the library. He drove to the nearest restaurant--another diner--and ordered a soup and salad; he knew he had to eat, but he wasn't very hungry.

The food wasn't nearly as good as the sandwich at Ruby's. But it was food, and he felt full enough and comfortable enough to pull into the rest stop, park in the farthest spot from the entrance, and turn in a bit early for the night.

It couldn't have been much past ten when his phone rang, but it woke him out of a sound sleep. He groped for the phone, but it continued ringing, and he stumbled to the front of the van where it lay on the seat where he'd left it. He didn't recognize the number.

"Hello?"

"Mr. Moore?" The voice was fairly young; Russ didn't recognize it, either. A girl. She sounded upset.

"Yes," Russ said. "Have we met?"

"At lunchtime," the girl said. "At the diner. I'm Ruby's daughter Paige."

"Does Ruby know you're calling me?" Russ asked immediately, because he wasn't about to get in between mother and daughter, not because of what he had offered to do.

"She told me to call," Paige said. "She wants you to come back, under cover of darkness, and strengthen the wards. She said no one else needs to know. Will you come?"

"Can I talk to Ruby first?" Russ asked.

"She...She's not here," Paige said, quickly; unhappily. "She...she had to go out. You'll come, won't you?"

She sounded far too worried and upset for this to be an honest call. The back of Russ' neck prickled. "Listen to me," he said, his voice soft, because he didn't know if anyone was listening in. "I need to know why you're so upset. I'm going to ask you a question, and you answer--BLT for yes and Lemon Meringue for no. Okay?"

He took her silence for assent. "Are the Hunters there?"

"No, you had a BLT for lunch," Paige said. "And french fries."

Russ' heart sank. "Have they broken through the wards yet?" But that was a stupid question; why else would she be so upset?

"You said the BLT was one of the best you'd ever eaten," Paige said softly.

They must have seen him leave without strengthening the wards. That was the only explanation. Russ closed his eyes. Had they followed him somehow? Or had they been waiting for this moment for the past eight months?

"Is your mother still alive?" How long would they allow her to answer these questions without realizing she was speaking in code?

Paige hesitated. "I...I don't remember what you had to drink. Iced tea? No...No, coffee. That's right. Black."

Russ took that to mean she didn't know or wasn't certain. "Are you alone?"

"You had lemon meringue pie for dessert," she said promptly, as if she'd expected that question. "Will you come? Please?"

"Yes, of course," Russ said. "I'm almost an hour away, but I'll get there as fast as I can. And I'll help. Just...just try to stay alive until I get there, okay?"

"Oh, thank you," she said, and she was crying now. "Thank you."

The phone went dead.

Grimly, Russ started his van, pulled out of the rest stop, and sped into the night.

Chapter 2

He did not call Ethan, because he was, of course, driving right into a trap. And Ethan would have protested, or tried to convince him not to go, or something else, and Russ would have refused, and asking forgiveness was much easier than asking for permission, after all.

He was driving into a trap, but he wasn't driving into it blind. He had more than one trick up his sleeve; more than one spell. Certainly, most of what he'd learned across his entire life had been to *combat* vampires, not help them, but it only took a little thought to switch most of that around.

And if this was an outright attack, Andre would be there. Russ would have bet his life on that.

He activated every single ward he'd ever placed on the van as he approached Ruby's village, and sailed through the perimeter wards without any ripples at all.

The lights across the dashboard had once only shown the presence of vampires; now they showed both. Humans were harder to track. He was still working on that. But Hunters normally carried certain items with them-- garlic, silver, stakes, among others--and that made them different than normal humans. He plugged in Paige's number on his handheld computer to track *that*, at least, and drove to the diner while the computer worked.

There was no outward sign of an attack, anywhere. The streets were empty, there were no obviously out-of-place cars or vans until Russ cast a spell, and saw the familiar Hunter vans clustered around the diner, hidden from view to anyone who didn't know the key to their wards.

His first thought was sabotage, to slice the tires or damage the engines somehow, but then he saw a silhouette in the diner window, barely lit by the emergency lights.

A guard, of course.

He drove around the back. There'd be a delivery entrance that would probably lead to the kitchen, and there was one, the door hung open, and there was a body lying in the parking lot.

Russ emerged from the van cautiously and approached the body. It wasn't a vampire, but a Hunter, and not one he recognized. *Score one*, he thought, and slipped inside.

The vampires had not killed the Hunter without casualties themselves. There was a vampire lying on the floor in front of the kitchen sink, and another one slumped against the stove. Why had they left the door open? Russ turned to close it just as a Hunter stepped inside.

Before he could react, the vampires attacked. The two of them had been playing dead. And they worked in tandem; this was obviously long rehearsed. Prudently, Russ stepped out of the way until the Hunter was dead.

Up until then, neither vampire had spoken, but as soon as the Hunter's body slumped to the floor, the closest one said, "There's someone else here."

Before they could find him, Russ left them to their hunt and slipped out of the kitchen and into the hallway. He didn't want to have to try to explain his presence to someone who did not know him; hopefully Ruby was in the building. Hopefully, Ruby was alive.

There were voices up ahead; Russ paused in the hallway to glance down at his handheld, which told him they were mostly vampires. And the number Paige had called from was two streets away. A house. According to the county auditor's website, it was owned by a man named Herman Jurgenson. A quick search of that name on the internet turned up nothing, but a search of the phone number turned up a 'for rent' posting three months before.

Since there weren't many humans present, and the diner itself seemed to be full of vampires, where had the humans in Ruby's family gone? As soon as that question presented itself, Russ knew the answer. Of course the Hunters would go after the weakest first. Not all of the humans in a vampire's household were wizards, after all.

Armed with what scant information he'd managed to glean, he stepped into the main room of the diner.

All the tables had been pushed away and piled against the wall. There were wounded; ten vampires, some suffering from silver poisoning, some burned, two who might have been dead.

And there were walking wounded, too. Ruby's left arm was in a sling, her shirt stained with blood. Two other vampires were limping. The rest seemed to be whole, at least for the moment.

There were three dead Hunters lying against the wall. The holes in their throats; on their wrists, perhaps even elsewhere, told Russ everything he needed to know.

Vampires didn't normally take prisoners, after all.

And he realized that they were more likely to attack first and ask questions later if he dropped his wards and exposed himself to them, but they would also sense his presence eventually. There was no simple way to do this.

"Any word?" Ruby asked for what seemed to be the thousandth time, because no one really answered her question. She paced, back and forth, back and forth. "Surely they wouldn't quietly kill *everyone;* they'd want to make some sort of show of power, wouldn't they?"

"An hour ago, she was still alive," Russ said, keeping his back against the wall, standing away from the other vampires and closest to Ruby herself, since she was the one less likely to kill him. "She called me. They *made* her call me."

There was a heartbeat of utter silence, and then Ruby had him up against the wall, her injury the only thing preventing her from killing him immediately. Russ' hands were around her wrist; *her* hand was around his throat, but he knew he couldn't stop her from strangling him, even with one hand. Not unless he resorted to Hunter tricks, and he didn't want to do that, because Hunter tricks normally ended in the death of the vampire.

"Tell me why I shouldn't kill you right now," Ruby snarled.

"Because she was still alive an hour ago," Russ managed to say, even though she was cutting off most of his air. "And I traced the call to a house two streets over from here. And if that's where they're keeping your family members, then you have the advantage now, because you know where they are."

"How did she have your number?" Ruby asked, and the pressure did not lessen.

"My card," Russ croaked. "It's on my card."

She released him, then, and stepped away. And then, quite deliberately, she rammed her fist through the plaster wall, right next to Russ' head. Russ didn't even have a chance to flinch, because he truly did not see her strike. She moved too fast.

That was why Hunters tended to rely on the advantage of surprise, because they had no other advantages against vampires, and both sides knew it.

"Speak," she said. "And then I'll decide if I will let you live. Are my guards dead?"

"They'd just killed another Hunter when I went past," Russ said, which was the truth. Two vampires left to check, he supposed; but in that respect, at least, he had nothing to hide. "1910 Honeysuckle Street. According to the auditor's website, it's a two-story house built in 1914. Frame construction. Colonial style. Seven rooms."

"Eight months ago, they locked all the humans of the Warren House in the basement and set the house on fire," one of the other vampires said, her voice soft.

"Yes, I know," Russ said. "That's why I'm trying to help you protect yourselves from them. Not for any glory on my part."

"Paige called you?" Ruby asked. "What did she say?"

"She told me you had changed your mind, and wanted me to come to strengthen the wards under cover of darkness so no one else would know. But she was too upset for it to be a legitimate call, so I devised a code so she could answer some questions without raising their suspicions."

"What kind of code?" Ruby asked.

"BLT for yes, Lemon meringue for no," Russ said. "She didn't know if you were still alive, she wasn't alone, and the Hunters were there with her."

"So you deliberately walked right into a trap?" One of the other vampires asked. "Why?"

"So what happened to the Warren Household doesn't happen here," Russ told them all, and something in his voice, or perhaps something in his bearing must have convinced them, because even Ruby nodded.

"Okay, then," she said. "They were alive an hour ago. We know where they are. How many Hunters have we killed?"

"Six," one of the vampires who had left said as he returned.

"How many are likely to be here?" Ruby asked Russ.

"No more than twelve," Russ said. "If this is to be a massive operation. If they're trying to annihilate everyone loyal to you in this entire town."

"A 'massive operation' is a dozen Hunters?" one of the other vampires asked in disbelief.

"I used to work by myself," Russ said, and they digested this silently, at least until Ruby spoke again.

"We can't outright attack the house," she said. "They're likely to kill them before we can get inside."

"One person, maybe even two, has a better chance of getting inside," Russ said.

"Are you volunteering?" Ruby asked with a hint of scorn in her tone of voice.

"I got in here," Russ said simply.

"I'm not willing to put the lives of every human in my household in your hands," Ruby said. "A year ago, you would have been out there with them."

"A year ago, my wife and my baby daughter were still alive," Russ said, and she stared at him, fiercely, then nodded.

"Go."

Chapter 3

1910 Honeysuckle Street was a white frame colonial style house with large, original windows and peeling paint. The lawn was overgrown; the bushes untrimmed. That made it easy to hide and harder to defend; Russ parked down the street a little ways and entered the yard on foot.

At first, he saw no sign of habitation. The windows were dark, the curtains drawn. But the wards around the house were very active, and when he read them, he realized what the Hunters had done.

There were ways, of course, to tie the strength of your wards to yourself, or others. It wasn't advisable to do so, because if the wards were breeched, the backlash could kill you, and that's what these Hunters had expected. They deliberately made the wards weak enough to destroy, which would, in turn, kill anyone tied to them, by force or otherwise.

They'd expected the vampires to attack, and their prisoners would die as soon as the wards fell.

Russ took ten precious minutes to anchor the wards to the vegetation and not the lives inside. It was exacting work, but he knew what he was doing and he did it quickly, thoroughly, so as not to lose the lives inside. And then, he blocked the exit, because the Hunters inside would not be escaping.

Not while he still lived, of course.

He didn't think Andre was with them. Andre was smart enough to expect Russ' actions, and smart enough to figure out a way to set a trap within a trap, perhaps, or even multiple traps as he progressed into the house.

But he had no real choice, so he stepped past the wards and continued across the lawn, tense for any sign that he'd been spotted.

It was actually easier to hide his presence from vampires than from humans.

The house had a basement, with a double outside door down a short set of stairs. It wasn't a new door, or secured very well at all. Russ was fairly sheltered at the bottom of the stairs, and he peered through the crack in the doors and into the basement; it was a cellar more than a basement, really, and there were people inside of it. Humans.

And one vampire, lying quite still against the wall. They only had what light their wizards could give them, which wasn't much, and Russ saw why a moment later.

He had wondered why the humans had not fought back during the attack on the Warren household. Oh, they'd fought, for a little while, at least, but then they had meekly trooped into the basement to die from the fire less than an hour later. Ethan hadn't tried to find out. Russ had, but no one seemed to know.

There were wounded here, too, and two Hunters as guards. Russ saw Paige, evidently unhurt, seated beside the vampire. Of the dozen or so humans in the room, most were young, in their teens yet, or early twenties.

They'd separated the age groups. No doubt the younger children were upstairs, the adults somewhere else. The threat would be, of course, death at any sign of trouble. Any sign of fight. And perhaps some were already dead.

Russ saw a couple unmoving figures lying past the light, stretched out on the floor, as if to remind them what happened if you tried to resist.

Any sign of trouble would set off a chain reaction.

There was a baby monitor on the floor in front of the little group. To let them listen when their little sisters or brothers or cousins or even, perhaps, children, were murdered.

Or parents, he thought, as a door opened up above and a body was shoved down the stairs.

One of the girls screamed, perhaps recognizing the body. The others swarmed to protect her; Paige stepped in front of the Hunters--brave, Russ thought--but they seemed more amused by the distress than inclined to kill anyone quite yet. Although one of them did shoot the vampire with one of those little crossbow bolts Russ had liked to use, he could only hope that the vampire was already dead.

In the chaos, Russ unlocked the door and slipped inside. The door was in shadow, so he doubted the Hunters would notice; their prisoners were shouting now, angry, the body had been dragged away by one of the boys.

Paige noticed the crossbow bolt the same time she saw the door swing open just enough to let Russ through. But she did not give him away; she dropped to her knees beside the vampire and said, angrily, "Haven't you done enough to him?"

"Not nearly enough," the Hunter with the crossbow said. "It's a shame I didn't bring any silver." This was not astounding; the Hunters wouldn't waste silver on humans, after all, and this vampire had obviously been in the wrong place at the wrong time.

"I brought some," the other Hunter said, and pulled out a little vial Russ also remembered; silver dust, suspended in oil. Very potent, very deadly. The vials were enspelled to explode on impact and shower anyone nearby with the contents. "And I could have you force him to drink it, girl."

"I would refuse," Paige said, and raised her chin in defiance.

"Then you would die, and we'd keep going until someone was willing to do it," the other Hunter said implacably.

The girl who had screamed was still crying, her sobs muffled.

Russ deliberately knocked over a pile of scrap wood; it clattered on the floor. And both Hunters glanced his way, and both Hunters saw the open door at the same moment. And he saw identical expressions on their faces; the realization that something had just gone terribly wrong, at least for them.

Two things happened at once. Russ dropped his wards and the other Hunter, the one with the vial, raised his hand to throw it to the ground. One of the boys jumped up to stop him--

"If it falls, it will explode," Russ said, and one of the girls spoke a spell so fast she almost pronounced it wrong. But she didn't, and the vial flew to her hand, unbroken.

Paige stood up, the bloody crossbow bolt in one hand. "We need their blood," she said furiously, sounding like her mother.

"They'll have other weapons," Russ said, and secured their new prisoners; both Hunters were staring at him, stunned by his appearance. "I guess the ones upstairs didn't bother to tell you they had Paige call me an hour ago?" He didn't allow them to answer. There were too many variables in spellcasting to allow them to speak.

Methodically, they stripped the Hunters of their weapons and their poisons. There weren't quite enough weapons to go around, but Russ made sure the ones who looked most capable had at least one weapon.

"I wouldn't give him their blood to drink," Russ said. "Not for a few days, at least. They'll have eaten a lot of garlic. It wouldn't kill him, but it would make him sick."

Paige nodded. "Is my mother alive?"

"She was twenty minutes ago," Russ said. "She sent me here to rescue you. The wounded should leave now; anyone who can't fight needs to get out of here fast. Are there safehouses nearby?"

"A block or two over," one of the boys said. Two others were donating blood to the vampire, who seemed to be drinking; his eyes were still closed, his visible skin tinged with gray.

"What did they do to him?" Russ asked, since his shirt was sodden with blood.

"They stabbed him when he tried to protect us," the sobbing girl whispered. "And they kicked him and beat him and made us watch. And they--"

"Did they use silver?" Russ asked gently.

"I don't think so," Paige said, and glared at the two Hunters. "I think we should kill them both."

"I'm not disagreeing with you," Russ said. "But we only have a small window to work in, and I want the wounded safe first. How many can't walk?"

They worked out a quick system; Russ enveloped them in wards and spells and led them all out to his van. The only one who couldn't walk was the vampire, so they lowered him down to the bed and Russ drove the others to the safehouse less than two blocks away. Five of them stayed behind, including Paige, by her insistence.

Evidently, Ruby had notified the ones in the safehouse that he might be coming, because they were expecting him. And he made them promise to tell Ruby that Paige was alive; he certainly didn't want to leave them wondering.

When he returned to the house less than ten minutes later, nothing had changed, but the tension in the basement had risen perceptibly. The baby monitor was squawking loudly; someone was crying. And someone else was shouting, but Russ couldn't make out the words.

"The Hunters use the element of surprise to catch their prey unawares," he said. "We're going to have to do the same thing. I can't ward each of you as thoroughly as my personal wards, but I can extend them to you if we're all holding hands. If you're at all squeamish about killing someone, now is the time to say. No one will think badly of you if you stay behind. The prisoners need to be watched, so someone *should* stay down here." He meant that someone to be Paige, but no one volunteered.

"Someone has to stay," Russ said again. "Paige, will you stay?"

Paige folded her arms. "You only want me to stay because of my mother," she said.

"That's true," Russ told her, seeing no reason to lie. "Because she would kill me if you died under my watch, and I'd rather get out of this alive."

One of the captive Hunters--the one with the vial, not the one with the crossbow--seemed to want to talk; Russ removed the spell preventing him from speaking, ready to replace it at any moment. "You can talk if you tell me something helpful," he said. "Try any spells, and I'll let them cut out your vocal cords after I'm done with you."

"You're Russell Moore," he said. "The traitor."

"I'm Russell Moore, yes," Russ said. "A smarter person than I was a year ago. If being a traitor means I'm saving lives, then so be it."

"They will kill you once they're done with us," the Hunter said, struggling against the bindings Russ had placed on them both. "They'll kill you!"

"Nothing helpful," one of the boys said, and replaced the spell before Russ could do it himself. "I'm Eric." He nodded to the other boys, "Cameron and Diego." And the other girl, "Samantha."

"How many of you are wizards?" Russ asked, and only Cameron and Eric raised their hands. "Okay then. Paige, Cameron, and Eric, come with me. Samantha and Diego, stay here and watch our prisoners. If anyone comes through the basement door and you don't know who they are, shoot them. Or hide."

They nodded, their eyes wide.

Russ held out his hand. "We'll have to hold hands for this to work," he said, and Cameron, Eric, and Paige joined hands. Paige held out her hand to him, and he activated his wards. "Be ready. Don't hesitate, no matter what you might see." He hesitated. "Even if it's one of your parents up there. Okay?"

Cameron and Eric nodded. Paige set her jaw. "Okay."

They walked up the stairs.

The door wasn't locked--why lock it?--and the basement came out into the kitchen, as Russ had suspected. There was no one in the kitchen, but Russ heard the crying child somewhere nearby; and someone murmuring to hush it. The shouting had stopped.

Silently, he directed Cameron, who was on the end, to close the door. And then, as one, they moved down the hall and into what would have been the living room.

The adults were here, and so were the children. Seven adults--two men, five women. The men were either unconscious or dead; the only woman standing was the one rocking the child. The children, none over the age of nine, sat huddled against the wall, their faces white. Shocked. But they were relatively unharmed, and there were ten of them, counting the crying one.

There were four Hunters. Russ raised his crossbow. Cameron raised his. They fired in tandem; two Hunters fell before the others even realized they were under attack. And then he dropped the wards, and Paige took care of the third Hunter; by then, the fourth had tried to flee, and one of the men had roused himself enough to stop him.

"Is there anyone else?" Russ asked. "Upstairs?"

"What about downstairs?" The man who had stopped the last Hunter tried to get up, but sank back down.

"They're at the safehouse," Paige said. "We took them there first. There were a lot of wounded."

"What about Kevin?" the woman with the child asked.

"He's alive," Paige said, and glanced at Russ. "They didn't use silver."

"No, they didn't," Russ confirmed, and both the woman and the man seemed relieved at the news.

"There's no one else," the man said. "Unless someone came in later. There were six Hunters--"

"Two are prisoners downstairs," Paige said. "They're secure."

"Why didn't you kill them?" the man asked, almost sharply.

"We thought rescuing you was more important," Eric said. "And in case there are others, we'd better go."

There were more dead upstairs. Three of the women and the other man. Two of the women had to be carried out; the children were the only ones not physically wounded. Russ pretended not to see when the man, who had not given his name, limped down the basement steps and returned with Samantha and Diego and a knife, which he washed off in the kitchen sink. Russ delivered them all to the safehouse, then, with Paige riding beside him and Eric and Cameron in the back, drove back to the diner.

There were two more bodies outside now, all Hunters. That made nine, total. As soon as he managed, he cornered Ruby and asked, "How did they get past your wards?"

"I wondered the same thing," Ruby said. "I owe you for this, Russell Moore."

Russ shook his head. "Just let me help you. That will be payment enough." He hesitated, not certain how she would react to what he suspected. "The wards were still active when I came through. The Hunters didn't tear them down. Someone let them inside."

"Yes." Ruby didn't seem surprised about this, only resigned. Sad, perhaps. "I'll find out who did it."

"I know you will," Russ said.

"It's a terrible thing when someone hands over their own family to the Hunters," Ruby said. "I'm *not* a terrible person."

"I'm glad you don't think that I let them in," Russ said. "I thought you might--"

"So you could return victorious, the hero of the day?" Ruby asked. "Yes, I considered it. But only for a moment." She smiled. "You're not the type. You're..." She paused, cocked her head. Started to turn. "Do you smell--"

The explosion seemed to happen in slow motion. Russ hadn't smelled a thing, but vampire senses were much more advanced. The wall buckled; a great wash of heat swept over him as he flew backwards and slammed into something, a table, perhaps. And a table was what saved him, because when he could hear again, when he could see--*barely* see; there was blood running down his forehead from a cut--he found himself lying against two of them, one overtop, one in front. And there was rubble everywhere. And screaming. Someone was screaming.

He tried to get up and fell back down. His ears were ringing, or was the alarm? He saw shadows--three of them, one limping--moving among the smoking debris.

The screaming abruptly stopped. Russ narrowed his eyes, trying to see the three figures past the smoke. They looked familiar, somehow. They looked...

And then he knew. The two captive Hunters. The man who had gone down to the basement, the man who had supposedly killed them. He'd *assumed* that. He hadn't checked. Why would he? He had no reason to suspect a wounded victim of betrayal.

He tried to get up again. His legs didn't want to work. Neither did his arms. And the room...well, it wasn't a room anymore, really, kept swaying around his head. The *world* kept swaying.

They were killing the wounded, he realized a moment later. They were methodically uncovering the dead or merely wounded, and they were killing them with one blow. Vampires and humans alike.

One shot from those damned little crossbows. Russ doubted they were hoarding their silver now.

But there was smoke, and wavering shapes in the smoke, and although Russ couldn't sort out his arms and legs to actually move to warn anyone, much less cast a spell. He tried, but the table moved and rubble rained down on his head and he realized that he wasn't quite as hidden as he had thought when they turned towards him.

And he had no means to defend himself, not wounded like this--and he still had no idea how badly he was hurt--when they moved the table and a pile of rubble and reached into the space it had made to pull him out.

One of the Hunters said something. Russ couldn't comprehend the muddled words even as he saw the man's lips move. The other Hunter raised his crossbow; Russ braced for death, but then the ground rumbled. Again. A secondary explosion. Hot air billowed out over the rubble. Flames. Black smoke.

Russ, already on the ground, was spared most of the destruction. The Hunters scattered; the wounded man disappeared.

After a little while, drifting, Russ realized he could hear again, after a sorts. The crackle of flames, nearby. Voices, also, nearby, but those were muffled, hidden by the smoke and the flames. His head was clearer, at least until he tried to move; pain shot up every joint when he tried to make his arms and legs work properly.

He didn't think he was dying, at least not yet.

A splatter of rain--water from a fire hose?--soaked his immediate area; the fire sizzled in protest.

Russ managed to roll over. He pushed himself upright against what had once been a wall and was now a pile of rubble. He was bleeding from dozens of cuts from broken glass, but he couldn't feel a thing. His shirt, shredded. His pants were no better.

There was an awful lot of blood.

It didn't hurt to breathe, but he felt something wrong inside his chest nonetheless. But at least he was breathing; the wounded man, the traitor, lay a few feet away, and he was definitely *not* breathing, at least not anymore.

Walking seemed to be beyond him, so he sat instead, since the fire hose had doused the immediate fire.

The ground rumbled again. Loose chunks of rubble broke loose from the piles; Russ watched as a hand appeared, not far away, uncovered by the shaking. He crawled, then. And methodically began to uncover the body.

At first, he thought he was spending his time on a corpse, but then the hand clenched, and scrabbled weakly at the rubble; and Russ spoke for the first time since the explosion.

"It's Russ," he said. "I'm right outside. I'll get you out."

And he had no idea it was Ruby until he uncovered her upper body all the way and she was pinned by a large slab of the roof, or a wall, or something, and he could not move that, not even with magic.

And he was just about to tell her that, to promise he'd find his way out of the mess to find someone to help when he felt a prick against his back and then, without a single word, the Hunter pulled the trigger.

He fell forward, onto Ruby. Rolled over; he couldn't catch his breath now; a tearing pain across his chest, his back prevented him from speaking. Methodically, the Hunter reloaded; methodically, he shot again.

They were not fatal shots by themselves. And Russ truly didn't realize what the Hunter intended until the man pulled out a dagger and plunged it into Russ' upper arm; and when Ruby's hand closed over that arm a moment later, a viselike grip.

The scent of human blood hung heavy on the air.

"*This* is what you are helping," the Hunter said, then glanced back and vanished into the quickly fading smoke.

Russ tried to struggle. Tried to speak. But it was useless; the first shot had stolen his breath, the second the numbness that had sheltered him from the pain.

And Ruby was wounded. Perhaps badly.

And vampires needed blood to heal.

She fed on the wound in his shoulder first, and then moved up to the vein in his neck. And Russ could not stop her.

He could not stop her. And that was exactly what the Hunter had intended.

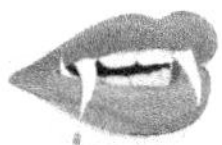

The next sound he heard was Ruby's voice, cursing. She had quite the vocabulary of curses. He lost a bit of time when she pulled out both bolts; the pain was enormous and swallowed him whole.

The cursing continued, unabated. And then, something wet and thick and hot trickled down the back of his throat. Trickled, and then gushed, filling his mouth with the taste of copper and iron. He would have choked on it if he could remember how to breathe. But his body remembered how to swallow, and his mind--what was left of it--knew what he was swallowing.

There wasn't enough of his mind left to rebel, so he swallowed.

The fire hose passed over them once again. And then, he heard a voice, echoing strangely in his head.

And Ruby said in reply, "Haven't you done enough?" And she said something else, but Russ didn't hear it, because the only link he had to life vanished then; his mouth filled with water, not...not blood, and he felt a weight on his chest that had nothing to do with rubble or the explosion.

Someone pulled the weight off his chest. Someone else pried open his eyes and shone a light into them, or perhaps it was the same person, because Russ was drifting now, lost in a sea of darkness.

You're dying, his mind supplied.

He expected them to do something, to cut off his head or stake him, just in case he'd come back, but they did not. They checked for a pulse, seemed satisfied when they didn't find one.

Another explosion rocked the area, this one farther away.

The safehouse, Russ' mind informed him in a dry, featureless voice.

Even though he was dying, after a little while he managed to open his eyes. And even though he was dying, he somehow pushed his body up to a sitting position.

Ruby lay beside him. She wasn't dying. She was dead.

Almost as if a beam of light had pierced the darkness surrounding him, Russ saw his van, not twenty feet away, still parked at the back of where the diner had been. A little singed, but unharmed.

He didn't see anyone else. There were lights elsewhere, shouts, screams. More water sluicing through the air.

He touched his wounds through his ruined shirt. They didn't seem to be bleeding anymore. His mind did not want to comprehend what that might mean.

Somehow, even though he was dying, he crawled. He crawled the twenty feet through rubble and water and soot and ash and broken glass, and he--somehow--made it to his van.

He thought he must have lost time for a little while after he dragged himself inside, because the next thing he remembered was waking up in the driver's seat with absolutely no memory of how he'd managed to drive in this state, half dead, wholly dying.

And he was on the interstate, driving.

He had no idea where he was going, but something in his subconscious seemed to know, and some piece of his talent was intent on keeping him alive long enough for something, at least. So he surrendered, because he couldn't think of anything else to do.

It was almost dawn when he arrived at Ethan's compound. The sky was grey, not black, when he drove down the gravel driveway to Ethan's house. He knew they'd see him coming; knew that the wards would recognize his van. When he stopped, Niles and Ethan ran out of the house to meet him.

It could have been a trap, Russ' mind thought. *You'll have to tell him to be more careful.*

They would have heard some of what had happened, of course. Perhaps they'd heard Russ was dead.

That last little thread of strength; that piece of himself that had sustained him across the miles, gave way with a little sigh; just a parting, like a piece of string that had been rubbed against a rough surface for far too long.

When they opened the driver's side door, Russ fell into Ethan's arms.

And perhaps, in that respect, it was a good thing Ethan was a vampire, because he knew--immediately, just by looking at Russ--most of what had happened.

And then there was a flurry. Russ saw Dolly, and Emily, only briefly, and others, just glimpses. It was mostly Ethan and Aden and Niles. And Ethan, shouting. Urgent. Desperate for something. Russ didn't realize he was trying to beat the dawn until they forced the first draught down his throat. It wasn't just one person's blood, but a mixture, vampire *and* human, and other things as well, a soup, of sorts, a potion...and then again, and again and again.

Russ had no strength to fight them, or to protest. He had nothing left at all.

His body recognized dawn as the sun rose. There was some knowledge in the back of his mind now; some realization of the time. And the cup withdrew from his lips. Someone gently closed his eyes, even though he could no longer see.

And he slept. Oh, he slept. He slept like the dead, without dreams.

Chapter 4

He awoke to someone reading a fairy tale, out loud. *The Princess and the Pea.* She was almost halfway through the story; Emily, of course, reading softly, very close by, as if not to disturb anyone else.

And there were others in the room. Even without opening his eyes, Russ sensed Ethan, and Aden, and Niles. Niles was asleep, lying on the floor with a pillow and a blanket. Ethan was sitting in a chair. Not the paisley chair, Russ thought; this wasn't the house they'd brought him to the first time. This was Ethan's actual dwelling place, where he'd spent a few blissful months less than a year before.

Aden sat in his chair, of course, tapping the arm with a pen or something that made a little clacking noise every time it hit the edge.

After a little while of this, when Emily had finished the story and started on another one, Ethan said, "Would you mind?"

There was no reproach in his voice, just weariness, but the clacking sound stopped.

Russ decided it was time to open his eyes, so he did. Ethan actually jumped in surprise; Emily's mouth dropped open; Aden stared at Ethan, not Russ, a question in his gaze that Ethan ignored.

"Russ? Can you speak?" Ethan's voice was rough. Too emotional. As if he hadn't quite known what would happen when Russ awoke.

Russ' mouth was terribly dry. He licked his lips and tasted blood, but the taste awoke no craving, no urge. Did that mean--*What* did that mean, exactly?

"Am I..." His voice cracked. He closed his eyes to try again. "Coffee?"

"Coffee?" Emily repeated, confused.

"Head hurts," Russ whispered. "Coffee helps." He opened his eyes and squinted at Ethan. "I'm alive?"

"Niles, wake up," Aden said. "You're alive," he said to Russ. "You are definitely not dreaming."

Niles helped him sit up, although Russ wasn't sure he could *stay* sitting up, not without a bit more strength. A pile of pillows behind him helped a little bit; he leaned back against them and tried to focus on the important question that he couldn't quite muster up enough courage to ask.

When Ethan returned with a mug of coffee and a thermos to boot, Russ couldn't even hold the cup himself. But it helped; his head cleared. Some of the fuzziness went away.

"Am I still human?" he asked the room at large, and everyone--*everyone*--looked to Ethan for an answer.

And Ethan hesitated, then met Russ' gaze squarely. "Yes," he said.

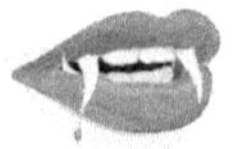

He'd been unconscious for an entire week. They'd been feeding him fluids, evidently, and Russ decided not to ask what *kind* of fluids he'd been drinking. Despite the lack of a Healer, however, his wounds had mysteriously healed.

After the first few hours of weakness, he'd recovered his strength. He felt...different.

He remembered Ruby's attempt to save him, and wondered if Ethan had done something similar.

But he had not awakened as a vampire.

After a little while, they told him what had happened. How Paige had not died in the initial attack. How she'd led retaliation against the Hunters, and how the last Hunters had not left the confines of Ruby's village, at least not while they were still alive.

Perhaps part of his mind had not believed Ethan's assurance that he was still human, because he held his breath the first time he ventured out into sunlight.

And he did not burn.

Paige had secured the wards against any additional Hunter attack. They'd initially thought Russ was dead as well, but then they'd discovered his van was missing, and hoped for the best. When someone finally thought to send a word of inquiry to Ethan, Russ hadn't awakened yet. Ethan prudently waited to send a reply.

There was one difference. A potion, Ethan said, that had saved his life. That he would have to drink for the rest of his life if he wanted to remain healthy and whole. It smelled revolting, and looked like blood. It was an ancient recipe, Ethan had told him, hesitating yet again.

Russ decided that Ethan wasn't quite telling the truth, but he wasn't quite lying, either. And he decided not to ask. He *almost* asked, but something in Ethan's gaze; something in his bearing, told him he probably would not like the answer.

After the destruction of Ruby's compound, after the other households heard from those who survived, Ethan's phone started ringing and would not stop.

Everyone wanted Russ to strengthen their wards. Everyone wanted to be safe. But the Hunters had to regroup as well; Russ knew they wouldn't arbitrarily attack so soon after losing so many men.

He went back to Ruby's compound first. Now Paige's compound, of course. They'd decided to rebuild the diner. He met with Paige, Cameron, Eric, and three of the surviving vampires in the basement of the new safehouse, and he told them what to expect. That the Hunters would not leave them alone. That they would have to be on guard until the Hunters were eliminated, or until someone managed to sign a truce between them.

That this, of course, was more than war. Now, it was personal.

Russ kept moving, always ahead of the Hunters, although there were some close calls. Every once in a while, when his supply ran low, Niles would show up with new bottles, or Ethan, or Dolly. Once, even Aden.

Once the households were secure, Russ turned to the solitary vampires, those who did not live in households, but usually lived among humans, hidden in plain sight, on residential streets, just like anyone else.

They were almost more paranoid than the ones who lived in households. And it was in one such house, three months after Ruby's death, three months after he woke up still a human, that he discovered that his blood could heal vampires of nearly every otherwise fatal wound.

It was supposed to happen like this:

Ethan called, or contacted a vampire household. Russ would then visit, strengthen their wards with his intimate knowledge of the Hunter's mode of operation, and leave.

But this--this changed everything.

The End

You can find ALL our books up on our website at:

http://www.writers-exchange.com

All Jennifer's books:

http://www.writers-exchange.com/Jennifer-St-Clair/

all our fantasy novels:

http://www.writers-exchange.com/category/genres/fantasy/

About the Author

Jennifer St. Clair grew up in Southern Ohio and spent most of her childhood in the woods around her home. She wrote her first novel when she was thirteen, and hasn't stopped since. She lives with her ball python, Fester, and two cats, Ash and Rowan.

In her spare time, she crochets, makes cloth dolls, collects antiques, books, and vintage clothing, and takes digital photographs with varying degrees of success.

Her *Beth-Hill series* is set in the area in America that contains many supernatural creatures: Wild Hunt, Vampires, Dragons, Faery and more.

It is part of the Universe that her *Jacob Lane Series, Karen Montgomery Series* and vampire trilogy, *The Shadow Series* are set in.

Follow all her books on her author page:

http://www.writers-exchange.com/Jennifer-St-Clair/

If you want to read more about other books by this author, they are listed on the following pages...

A Beth-Hill Novel (Stand Alone Novels)

Are creatures of the night and all manner of extramundane beings drawn to certain locations in the natural world? In the Midwestern village of Beth-Hill located in southern Ohio, the population is made up of its fair share of common citizens...and much more than its share of supernatural residents. Take a walk on the wild side in this unusual place where imagination meets reality.

Blood of Innocents

Ten years ago, Orien, crown prince of the Seleighe, was captured by his mortal enemies, locked in a dungeon and turned into a vampire. Six years into Orien's sentence, the Healer's brother Cullen disobeyed his mistress's orders to kill him and turned him into a vampire instead, thus sealing both their fates for all eternity.

Now both Orien and Cullen are set free. But a secret only Cullen knows lies locked inside his mind, threatening to drive him mad before he can uncover the identity of a traitor--the very elf who betrayed Orien and left them both to die in darkness.

Publisher: http://www.writers-exchange.com/blood-of-innocents/

Full Moon

Werewolves change into wolves when the moon is full. But Edward's curse only allows him to be *human* when the moon is full.

Alone and despairing, Edward hides himself away from the world. He's scraped out a meager existence for himself for almost a century in the forest he's grown to love and call home. But in the depths of a terrible winter, he stumbles across clues from the life his mother left behind in Faerie. The truth may give him the answers he needs about the source of his birthright... and the curse that holds him captive.

Publisher: http://www.writers-exchange.com/full-moon/

A Beth-Hill Novel: Jacob Lane Series

Are creatures of the night and all manner of extramundane beings drawn to certain locations in the natural world? In the Midwestern village of Beth-Hill located in southern Ohio, the population is made up of its fair share of common citizens...and much more than its share of supernatural residents.

Jacob Lane is a ten-year-old girl who's spent her life unaware of her magical heritage. After being sent to Darkbrook, a school of magic, supernatural mysteries seem to spring to life all around her and her new friends.

Book 1: The Tenth Ghost

After Jacob Lane's parents mysteriously vanish, she's sent to Darkbrook, the only school of magic in the United States. While there, she and her new friends stumble upon a series of mysterious deaths in the nine ghosts that haunt the halls of Darkbrook. These ghosts were students who died at the school over the past hundred years. Will Jacob become the tenth ghost, or can she stop a witch's reign of terror?

Publisher: http://www.writers-exchange.com/the-tenth-ghost/

Book 2: The Ninth Guest

When Jacob's friend Ophelia's family decides to open up their castle for guests, amateur paranormal sleuth Jacob Lane is invited to join in on the fun. "Spend the night in a vampire's castle and live to tell the tale!" is supposed to be a fundraiser to help Ophelia's family pay the bills. Heating a castle costs quite a bit, after all. But, after the truth of an old secret is uncovered, what began as an innocent business venture soon turns deadly when vampire hunters get involved.

For years, the vampire hunters have had only one goal: To destroy all vampires. With the help of a new friend, Jacob and Ophelia must work together to save the entire VonBriggle family from extinction.

Publisher: http://www.writers-exchange.com/the-ninth-guest/

Book 3: The Eighth Room

For two hundred years, the Selkies have kept themselves separate from those who live on land. But now the Selkies need allies or they'll be crushed by their ancient enemies, the Finfolk.

Jacob and Ophelia, students at the only school of magic in the United States, uncover a mystery that dates back to Darkbrook's beginnings. While helping clean out old storage rooms for classroom expansion, they find something that might save the Selkies from extinction. With the help of the youngest member of the Wild Hunt who are no longer so wild or terrifying, they must foil the Finfolk who desire the Selkie's destruction...or die trying.

Publisher: http://www.writers-exchange.com/the-eighth-room/

Book 4: The Seventh Secret

After a picture of Niklas, the dragons' liaison to the only school of magic in the United States, shows up in too many newspapers to count, Darkbrook is forced to go on the defensive. The secret of Darkbrook's existence has been discovered. But there are more than dragonhunters in the forest, and, as Jacob Lane, supernatural sleuth and student at Darkbrook, learns how to use her newly discovered talent of healing, she helps to right an old wrong and must battle a teenaged wizard intent on proving--once and for all--that magic is real.

Publisher: http://www.writers-exchange.com/the-seventh-secret/

Book 5: The Sixth Stone

Jacob Lane, supernatural sleuth, and Danny, her werewolf friend, stumble across an alternate world where the Wild Hunt was never bound, and Darkbrook, the school of magic they attend, was abandoned a hundred years ago.

But when the Hounds of the Hunt wish to surrender, the two students are swept up in a whirlwind of heartbreak, betrayal, and the discovery of a lost treasure.

Publisher: http://www.writers-exchange.com/the-sixth-stone/

A Beth-Hill Novella: Karen Montgomery Series

Are creatures of the night and all manner of extramundane beings drawn to certain locations in the natural world? In the Midwestern village of Beth-Hill located in southern Ohio, the population is made up of its fair share of common citizens...and much more than its share of supernatural residents. Take a walk on the wild side in this unusual place where imagination meets reality.

Karen Montgomery was an ordinary woman until she stumbled into the extraordinary... A bargain with elves worth its weight in gold. A plague of sinister ladybugs. Rogue vampire hunters, including one who tries to turn over a new leaf--with disastrous consequences. A ghostly huntsmen of the Wild Hunt wishing for redemption. Karen's life will never be the same again.

Book 1: Budget Cuts

Karen Montgomery is used to taking care of the unpleasant jobs no one else wants to deal with. When a shortage of funds forces her to fire fifteen employees from the library, she isn't happy, but the nasty task has to be done and she is, after all, the boss. But Karen finds finishing her task impossible when she can't seem to track down Ivy Bedinghaus, a night clerk she's never actually met. Once she finally does confront Ivy, she's thrust into a centuries-old conflict that makes her previous troubles radically pale in comparison.
Publisher: http://www.writers-exchange.com/budget-cuts/

Book 2: The Secret of Redemption

Karen Montgomery, librarian, finds herself embroiled in another otherworldly adventure...

A member of the Wild Hunt--ghostly myths that aren't so ghostly (or myth-like) anymore--needs help in reconciling who he once was in life and who he is now.

A little girl has gone missing. And the one most likely responsible for her disappearance is the one Karen must prove innocent.
Publisher: http://www.writers-exchange.com/the-secret-of-redemption/

Book 3: Ladybug, Ladybug

An innocent attempt to rid the library of a plague of ladybugs turns sinister when a rogue vampire hunter gets the contract for pest control.

Ivy Bedinghaus, who works for Karen as a night clerk--along with all the vampires in Beth-Hill--are in danger, and their only hope for survival is with the help of Karen, a member of the Wild Hunt, and Russell Moore, a reformed vampire hunter.

Publisher: http://www.writers-exchange.com/ladybug-ladybug/

Book 4: Detour

One wrong turn sends Karen down a road that shouldn't exist, to the site of an old accident and an even older mystery. With reformed vampire hunter Russell Moore's help, Karen finds the key to the mystery. But Russ keeps his own secrets...some of which are deadly.

When old friends from Russ' past come to call, Karen realizes his secrets might just mean his doom. After a terrible incident three years ago, before Karen met him, Russ wants only to live the rest of his life quietly in Beth-Hill. But his secret might not allow him the new lease on life Russ longs for.

Publisher: http://www.writers-exchange.com/detour/

Companion Story: Russ' Story: Capture

Long before Russell Moore ever met supernatural sleuth Karen Montgomery or set foot in Beth-Hill, he was a vampire hunter, possibly the best vampire hunter of all. He brought down whole nests of vampires, caring little about the consequences of his actions. Anyone who lived with or helped the vampires became enemies to be slaughtered.

So what kind of an idiot would capture a ruthless vampire hunter without a conscience and try to reform him?

Ethan Walker was that idiot. Wanting to protect his family, Ethan set out to prove to Russ that vampires weren't all evil, soulless creatures. If Russ would allow himself to witness their lives, see their humanity, surely he and other vampire hunters like him would let them live in peace. *Surely?*

Publisher: http://www.writers-exchange.com/capture/

Secrets When in Shadow Lie

Twelve years ago, Ryan Grey was cursed by a witch to hide a secret. He's lived with the curse of being unable to die permanently, and, over the years he's slowly losing the memory of his past until almost nothing remains.

But now, after a chance meeting with an elf named Zipporah, he discovers the key to unlocking the secret and breaking the curse once and for all...if he can survive the breaking.

Publisher: http://www.writers-exchange.com/secrets-when-in-shadow-lie/

The Dead Who Do Not Sleep

Will Spark only wants a good night's sleep after a night of drinking. Instead, two thugs bang on his door, demanding answers to questions he can't understand. And then they killed him...

Publisher: http://www.writers-exchange.com/the-dead-who-do-not-sleep/

A Beth-Hill Novel: The Abby Duncan Series

Are creatures of the night and all manner of extramundane beings drawn to certain locations in the natural world? In the Midwestern village of Beth-Hill located in southern Ohio, the population is made up of its fair share of common citizens...and much more than its share of supernatural residents. Take a walk on the wild side in this unusual place where imagination meets reality.

Situated in Beth-Hill, where imagination meets reality, is The Rose Emporium, owned by elderly and not-a-little-odd Rose Duncan. The large Victorian house smackdab in the middle of nowhere is a cross between a pawn shop and an antique store that caters to supernatural creatures needing to barter. Rose's twenty-something niece, Abby Duncan, discovers that the world isn't made up of just run-of-the-mill, ordinary humans but an entire spectrum of unusual beings. With her preconceptions about what's normal and what's not turned upside-down, Abby is in for a whole lot of startling truths, mysteries-- about herself and the people and places around her--and danger.

Novella 1: By Any Other Name

Woodturner Abby Duncan decides to sell her spindles at a local Renaissance Festival with only some success. After all, no one really spins their own yarn anymore, do they? While there, she discovers that one of her newfound friends is not what he appears--and his secret is about to get him killed!

Publisher: http://www.writers-exchange.com/by-any-other-name/

Book 2: The Uncrowned Queen

Abby Duncan's elderly Aunt Rose has always been a bit odd. And now she's off on a mysterious trip, leaving Abby behind to run the Rose Emporium, an unusual sort of antique shop. Such an extraordinary store would have been a perfect place for Seth and the others, her friends from the Renaissance Festival, to take a break from traveling between Faires. But when tragedy strikes and Abby and the others discover the true nature of the Rose Emporium, they'll have to travel into Faerie itself before their tightknit group is whole again.

Abby doesn't know much about her family history, but she's about to find out the truth...whether she likes it or not.

Publisher: http://www.writers-exchange.com/the-uncrowned-queen/

Book 3: Coming Soon!

A Beth-Hill Novel: The Shadows Trilogy

Are creatures of the night and all manner of extramundane beings drawn to certain locations in the natural world? In the Midwestern village of Beth-Hill located in southern Ohio, the population is made up of its fair share of common citizens...and much more than its share of supernatural residents. Take a walk on the wild side in this unusual place where imagination meets reality.

A Dreamer dreams the future when the past is not yet laid to rest. Ten years ago, a plague swept across the Seven Kingdoms. Ten years ago, the Queen of Iomar's son was exiled and named the author of the magical plague. Now, in the present, Terrin works to complete his ultimate goal: Control of the Seven Kingdoms using his son's power to supplement his own. But his attempt at dominion meets resistance and the fate of the world rests in the unlikely hands of an exiled prince, a Dreamer, and a vampire...

Book 1: The Prince of Shadows

When Alban's father Terrin appeared at the castle door with a vampire in tow and apologies on his lips, Alban fell under his spell just like everyone else and welcomed him home. But Terrin didn't return to live quietly in his brother's kingdom. He had other plans and, with Alban's untrained powers at his disposal, he begins his ruthless plan to destroy the Seven Kingdoms and rule them all, beginning with his brother's death.

Terrin engineers events to cast the blame on his nephew, Teluride, intending to see the boy executed for his father's murder. But there are those who would thwart Terrin in his mad plan for power, and Alban forms an unlikely alliance with Skade, the reclusive Queen of Iomar, and Terrin's slave, a young vampire with no memory of his name or origins. Although the future looks grim, Alban and the vampire attempt to stop Terrin...and they almost succeed.

A darker history lies at the heart of Terrin's treachery, and only Skade knows the true reason why Terrin would murder his own brother and attempt to destroy both Alban and the vampire to achieve his goals. The Ghost who resides in Skade's mirror--her servant and thrall--holds one of the keys to Terrin's madness. Unfortunately, more than one person wishes for the past to remain the past and the future to hold no shadows of what might have been...

Publisher: http://www.writers-exchange.com/the-prince-of-shadows/

Book 2: Lost In Shadows

Events set in motion ten years ago come to a head as Skade, the reclusive Queen of Iomar, and Nicodemus, who is imprisoned by Skade, struggle to free Alban and the vampire from Terrin's grasp. Old secrets come to light when Skade's exiled son is forced to face his past--or die trying to redeem himself once and for all. Can the crimes of the past truly be forgiven? Only time will tell...and time is running out.

Publisher: http://www.writers-exchange.com/lost-in-shadows/

Book 3: Bound In Shadows

With his power crushed, brother to the king and father to Alban, Terrin is forced to take drastic measures to regain his sons after they are freed and harness the power they possess. But he has an ally inside the healer's house where they are recovering who works to further his plans. The Queen of Iomar, Skade's son, courts redemption to try to save his mother's life, and the vampire who no longer remembers his own name dreams a dream that might save them all...or damn them if success is thwarted.

Publisher: http://www.writers-exchange.com/bound-in-shadows/

A Beth-Hill Novel: Wild Hunt Series

Are creatures of the night and all manner of extramundane beings drawn to certain locations in the natural world? In the Midwestern village of Beth-Hill located in southern Ohio, the population is made up of its fair share of common citizens...and much more than its share of supernatural residents. Take a walk on the wild side in this unusual place where imagination meets reality.

The Wild Hunt roamed the forest outside of Beth-Hill until the Council bound them for a hundred years. Nevertheless, a century of existence has made an indelible mark not easily forgotten for these ghostly myths that are no longer so ghostly or myth-like...

Book 1: Heart's Desire

The Wild Hunt roamed the forest outside of Beth-Hill until the Council bound them for a hundred years--a lifetime for a human but only a passing thought to one such as Gabriel, Master of the Wild Hunt. As the Council's binding draws to a close, old enemies reappear to ensure that the Wild Hunt is bound once more--to a creature much worse than the Council has been.

Publisher: http://www.writers-exchange.com/hearts-desire/

Book 2: Fire and Water

As a young vampire, Erialas Morgan brought his mother back to life with a spell that shouldn't exist, shouldn't have worked...perhaps shouldn't have been performed at all. Desperation and love are his only excuses for doing the unthinkable.

There are others who wish to use that same spell for their own gain--and to destroy the Wild Hunt once and for all. Caught in the middle of a war between the Morgan clan of vampires and their human kin, Erialas turns to the Hunt for help. But even Gabriel, the Master of the Wild Hunt, may not be able to stop the tide of death and destruction once it turns.

Publisher: http://www.writers-exchange.com/fire-and-water/

Book 3: The Lost

Almost sixty years ago, Darkbrook, the only school of magic in the United States, opened its doors to students of decidedly different natures, sending out letters of invitation to the elves, the dragons, and the vampires. The three who responded to the invitation banded together despite their differences but vanished only weeks later along with an entire classroom full of students and their teacher after a field trip gone horribly wrong.

The Wild Hunt has healed and the Hounds have grown closer together, keeping Darkbrook's forest safe and secure for those who live there. Malachi, one of the eldest members of the Wild Hunt, has adapted to Josiah's spell to help him see, but when a demon boy trapped in the body of a human body for sixty years inside the school disrupts the newfound calm, the Hunt--and those they protect--are thrust into a struggle that should have ended long ago when a vampire, an elf, and a dragon vanished into the Mists.

Publisher: http://www.writers-exchange.com/the-lost/

Book 4: A Glint of Silver

Jericho is a vampire who wants is to live away from the Richmond household of vampires led by his ruthless father Connor. When Jericho tries to escape, Connor punishes him and leaves him to die. Tristan is determined to be the one to bring Jericho back, but he can't see him suffer for wanting a normal life. As long as Connor lives, Jericho will never be safe or free. As long as Connor *lives*...

Publisher: http://www.writers-exchange.com/a-glint-of-silver/

Book 5: All That Glitters

As a member of the cruel Morgan Household of vampires, twelve-year-old Arthur Morgan has been abused all his life.

Maya, a water fairy, shows him just how horrible and twisted the household he's grown up is. With her help, and the unexpected help of an adult vampire, Arthur attempts to escape.

Can he become something more than what his father has decreed?

Publisher: http://www.writers-exchange.com/all-that-glitters/

The Chelsea Chronicles

Normally a quiet, serene place, Chelsea Kingdom seems like the perfect location for a centuries' old vampire to blend in and live a normal life, even escape hunters and an angry mob. Unfortunately, his timing couldn't be worse...

Book 1: So You Want to be a Vampire

Chelsea Kingdom is usually a pretty quiet place but recent murders--committed by a vampire--upset the calm. Newcomer to town, Vlad Dhalgren wants only to blend in and live a normal life. He quickly learns that isn't possible, given that other vampires have been hiding in the shadows around the castle--in plain sight--for years.

Despite her lineage, Anna Everett, the crown princess of the Kingdom of Chelsea, isn't a wizard like her father, which means she will never be Queen. She has only one friend, Valerian Moreton--Val--who has secrets he's never shared that could get him *and* Anna killed...

Publisher: http://www.writers-exchange.com/so-you-want-to-be-a-vampire/

Book 2: Transformation

As Anna, crown princess of Chelsea, adjusts to life as a vampire after recent events, Vlad plans for a future he has no real hope to seeing come to pass due to injuries sustained while attempting to save Anna's life. But, as life goes on for Anna and her friend Valerian "Val" Moreton, it changes for others--some of whom are not quite what they seem...

Publisher: http://www.writers-exchange.com/transformation/

You can find ALL our books on our website at:

http://www.writers-exchange.com

All Jennifer's books:

http://www.writers-exchange.com/Jennifer-St-Clair/

all our fantasy novels:

http://www.writers-exchange.com/category/genres/fantasy/